Margaret & Molly

A Mystery in Hawaii

By Sarah Evangeline Martin

Bezalel
Media

Margaret & Molly: A Mystery in Hawaii
by Sarah Evangeline Martin
©2022 Sarah Evangeline Martin
ISBN: 9798363797989
Printed in the United States of America
Cover Design & Illustrations by Gloria Vanessa Nicoli
Production Management by Inkling Creative Strategies
Published in the United States by Bezalel Media

To my wonderful family, and to the loving memory of my great-grandpa, Eugene Barton, and my Papa, Rev. Clinton Martin.

Chapter 1 - Art Class

It was a Friday afternoon after a long day of school, and my little sister and me (Margaret Mason) were in our last day of art class before summer break. I waited patiently in my seat for the class to begin. I was really excited about today because our art teacher, Ms. Gregory, had an announcement to make. I hoped that it would be something about a field trip. Eleven-year-old girls like me can get very excited about field trips.

Molly was impatiently wiggling in her seating. "Hey, Molly," I said in a slight southern accent. "Sit still. Ms. Gregory will be here soon."

"But I can't, Margaret," Molly whined in her southern drawl. "She's taking so long."

"Well, try to hold it together." I leaned back to my own spot. Ms. Gregory was at the front of the room in no time. "See?" I whispered to Molly.

My little sister smirked and flipped her shoulder-length, white blonde hair. She had the frizziest, curliest hair in all of Texas. Molly said it was all natural.

I fixed my eyes on Ms. Gregory as she welcomed us all. "Today we will be making foil animals and covering the outside with paper so that we can paint them," she said. That sounded so fun. I couldn't wait to get started, but what about the announcement?

Ms. Gregory soon answered my question when she said, "As you know, I do have an announcement to make after our class. But right now, let's focus on our art project."

She got up from her desk at the front of the room and handed out pieces of foil, paper, paints, stickers, and a lot more supplies to every kid. After she finished explaining how to do the project, everyone got started.

At first, I thought it would be a good

idea to do a unicorn, but that seemed a bit hard after I thought about it. Instead, I decided that I was going to make a bunny. I started on the fluffy tail, rolling the foil into a ball.

"What animal are you doing?" Molly asked.

"I'm making a bunny," I told her, setting the tail aside as I started on the body.

"Oh," Molly said. "Maybe I'll make that, too."

I sighed and kept working.

After I finished putting the pieces of foil together to make my bunny, I looked it over. The bunny's ears looked a little sad, but when I covered it in paper, it would look better.

I looked over at my little sister to see how she was doing. Molly's foil bunny was already finished and was half-way covered in paper. She stuck her tongue out to one side, looking really concentrated, and there was paint on her cheek and nose. There were also crayons spilled everywhere.

Uh-oh, I thought.

"Oh, Molly," I said. "What happened here?"

Molly looked up with an innocent look on her face. "What do you mean?"

Ms. Gregory walked up to our desks. "Oh my," she said. "Looks like we have quite the little art project going on over here."

"Sorry, Ms. Gregory," I said.

"That's okay. Molly's being very creative. What exactly are you making, Molly?" she asked.

"A bunny rabbit," Molly answered frankly.

"Indeed." Ms. Gregory smiled looking over at me this time. "And what about you, Margaret?"

"A bunny, too," I said with no expression at all.

"Oh." Ms. Gregory chuckled. "Well, I'll come back to you two in a moment. I'm just going to check the other students' work."

Soon we had finished and Ms. Gregory looked over everyone's completions. She complimented all the students no matter how their projects looked.

At the end of class before we were let out, Ms. Gregory stood at the front of the room to make her announcement. I was not expecting at all the thing I heard next.

Everyone listened quietly as Ms. Gregory began.

"I have been your art teacher for a very long time, and I love each and every one of you. But unfortunately, I will be stepping down soon."

There were gasps and chatter amongst everyone.

"Don't worry, children," she reassured. "I'll be here until summer break starts. After summer break, you will be given a new art teacher."

I was very sad about this announcement. Ms. Gregory was a wonderful art teacher. Why was she going away? I almost raised my hand to ask this question, but I decided that even if I knew why she was stepping down, it wouldn't change anything.

"Please remember to bring all of your projects home with you," Ms. Gregory reminded us.

As everyone packed up, Molly leaned over and whispered in my ear, "I wonder who the new art teacher's going to be."

Chapter 2 - Mom's Friend

When Molly and I got out of art class, I saw our mom's silver van parked out front. As we got closer, I realized that Mom wasn't in her car. Molly tugged on my sleeve and pointed across the parking lot. Mom was standing by a purple Jeep talking to a pretty, middle-aged woman. She had dark hair and a butter-colored skirt with matching earrings. I wondered who she was. I scanned my memory to see if I knew her. Nope. But obviously, my mom did. Molly began to walk over to them, so I followed.

"Hey Mom, we're done with our art class," Molly said.

Mom turned around. "Oh, hi Molly. Margaret. I'd like you to meet Miss Mary."

"Nice to meet you," the woman said politely. "You can call me Mary."

"Nice to meet you, too, ma'am," I answered. The woman held out her hand, and Molly and I took turns shaking it. At first, she smiled at us, but then, the smile quickly faded. It almost seemed like she was squinting at Molly and I, like she wanted to say something, or maybe ask a question.

After a few seconds, Mom turned to Miss Mary and motioned towards our van. "We should probably get going now. My husband will be home from work soon."

"Totally . . . sure. It was nice to see you," Miss Mary replied with a smile. Just before she left, she glanced at me one last time with a bit of a questioning look.

When she was gone, Molly crossed her arms. "Who is she?" she asked.

Mom looked distracted. "Who? Mary? Oh, she was my friend from high school."

"Oh," Molly said, twisting one of her ringlets as if she were in deep thought.

"Well, we need to get home. Hop in, y'all," Mom said as she threw her wavy strawberry blonde hair up into a ponytail.

On our way home, I told Mom that Ms. Gregory was stepping down.

"Oh, that's too bad," she replied. "But I'm sure they'll replace her with a wonderful new art teacher."

On the rest of the way home, I thought about Ms. Gregory stepping down and Mom's friend Miss Mary. Mom kind of quickly changed the subject when I'd asked about her friend. I'm not sure why, but I kind of felt a little suspicious about this Miss Mary. Maybe it was the way she was looking at Molly and me.

Soon, Mom pulled up to the driveway. "All right, we're home. Molly, Margaret, bring your art stuff in so that I can see the projects that you made."

Molly grabbed her pink and purple backpack and scurried up to the front door, but someone else opened it before she could. It was Dad. "Hey, y'all," he greeted. We use the word 'y'all' a lot since we live in Texas.

I smiled. "I'm glad you got to come

home from work early, Dad!"

Dad smiled back, "Me, too." He helped Molly hang her coat up. "Oh, by the way," he said, "I made Minestrone soup for dinner." We cheered and hurried inside.

When we sat down at the table Dad said grace, and then we dug into his delicious soup.

Chapter 3 - The Extra Fancy Party

I pushed my pink rocking chair to the foot of my desk, grabbed my homework that was spilling out of my worn purple backpack, and brought it to the desk. I was really excited for it to be summer break. Mom had said that we were going on a vacation this summer, and I couldn't wait to figure out where we were going.

Then, someone came running in wearing Mom's fancy straw hat, but it wasn't Mom. "Molly? What are you doing in here?" I asked.

Molly scampered across the floor to my closet and grabbed all my feather boas. What was she up to?

"Molly what are you doing? You have way more boas in your room than I do. Why do you need mine?"

Molly whirled around. "It's still a work in progress, M." She smiled, grabbed two more boas, and left, walking out with a spring in her step. With all of my boas. WHAT in the world could this girl possibly be doing with all of those boas?

I decided to do a little investigating. I knew I had homework to do, but it would have to wait.

I tiptoed to Molly's room and peeked in. I couldn't believe my eyes.

Pink, purple, green, blue, orange, red, silver, and gold boas were EVERYWHERE! On her bed, on her shelf, absolutely everywhere! Molly frowned at me. "What are you doing in here?"

"This place is a mess, Molly! What do you think you're doing?"

I was very unhappy about her messy room, mainly because I was moving into her room in just a few days. Last week Mom had decided that we should share a room. She said it would be good for us, but I also knew that she wanted to clear out a space for a guest room.

Molly put her hands in front of her and kicked some of the boas out of her way to get to me. "Just throwing a little party. Mom told me that we're going to Hawaii for vacation, so I wanted to host a Hawaiian luau."

My eyes widened. "We're going to Hawaii? Yippee!"

After my little burst of excitement, I turned my attention back to Molly and her luau. "But Molly, you can't just take all my boas without asking first."

Molly didn't answer. Instead, she picked up a piece of paper and began to scribble something on it.

"What are you doing now?" Molly finished and handed it to me. "What's this? Emma, Lola, Natasha, Jenny, Brooklyn? Are these party guests?"

Molly grinned. "Yes, and here's another list. Look." She gave me another paper and I opened it.

"Is this a food list? Also, another thing— does Mom know about this?"

Molly grinned mischievously. "Not yet."

"Well, you can't have a party without Mom's permission."

"It's not a party, it's a luau," Molly corrected, and then with a dramatic sniffle, she continued. "But I know." A smile appeared across her face. "And that is why I'm going to ask her right now." Molly ran down the stairs and went to the mud room.

"Molly, Mom's in the kitchen," I said, following her. Molly pulled on her blue rubber boots and opened the mud room cupboard door. She grabbed her orange binoculars. "First I need to find some flowers," she said, giggling.

"Flowers?" I asked with curiosity.

I put on my grey jean jacket and chased her to the daisy field behind our house on a sprawling, four-acre property. I finally caught up with her. "Wow, you're a fast runner."

Molly laughed. "Thanks."

"So, why are you picking flowers again? I thought you were going to ask Mom if you could have a party, or Hawaiian luau, or whatever?"

Molly gave a sneaky smile. "Yes. But I'm doing it the smart way."

I gave her a look. "The smart way?"

"Yeah," she said.

I didn't bother asking what "the smart way" was. But I soon found out.

Molly started picking flowers. For a few minutes I just watched her picking the flowers and humming a little tune. Then I started to pick flowers, too, and I helped her put a beautiful bouquet together. Once it was perfect, we both went back to the house. Then, Molly wrote Mom a love note while I tidied up Molly's room. Half the reason I did it was to collect all of my feather boas and make sure they made it back to my room.

Once they were put away in my closet safe and sound, I heard a happy noise coming from down the hall. I went to see what was going on. It was Molly with the biggest smile ever on her face. I grinned. "So Mom said yes?"

Molly grinned back. "Yep."

"Need any help with your luau?"

Molly put her finger to her chin.

I raised my eyebrows. "Anything?"

Molly gave me a little smile and then scratched her head like she was thinking, but I knew she really wasn't. She knew exactly what she wanted me to do.

I was starting to get a little anxious. Maybe I shouldn't have asked. "Well, come on, what is it?"

"Okay, okay, there's a couple things that you could help with."

"Well, put me to work."

"I'll make you a list," she said with an excited squeal.

"A list? There's that many things?"

Molly smirked. "Yes." Then she skipped away to write the list.

I stood there for almost ten minutes just waiting until Molly came back with a piece of paper in an origami fold, which she passed to me. "Since when did you learn how to do origami?"

"Art class. Don't you remember?"

"Ah, yes. It's a very nice, ummm . . . butterfly?"

Molly frowned.

"Elephant? Rat? Lizard?" Molly looked at me, and I knew I didn't guess right. "Gopher?" I said weakly and smiled.

Molly looked at me for a long time and finally said, "PIG."

"Pig. Yes, of course, it's a pig," I answered as though I had known all along.

I opened the origami. It was a long list with little green flowers drawn all around it.

#1 Get pink and purple paper cups and some strawberry ice tea.
#2 Get chocolate covered pretzels and a big orange bowl to put them in.
#3 Get 30 or 40 more feather boas from the dollar store.

Oh no, not going to happen, I thought. I read the rest of the list.

#4 Get cotton candy puff balls.

Cotton candy puff balls. The most sugar-filled, pink food coloring mess you could ever get your hands on. Mom would never go for Molly's plan for a sugar high for her and her friends at her party. "That's not going to happen either," I said to myself.

#5 Get us fancy jewelry boxes for our jewelry trade.

#6 Get some decorative fake luau flowers.

WOOOOOWWW. That was a lot of things she needed me to get. I didn't bother telling her that practically nothing on her list was Hawaiian-themed. I just shrugged, then went on my way to grab my bike and helmet. For better or worse, I would do what I could to help my little sister prepare for her fancy party.

—

I had been all over town on my bike, or at least that's what it felt like. My last stop was the party store. When I walked in, the place was filled with people. As I looked for the orange bowl Molly wanted, I started to think about the other day, about that lady Miss Mary who Mom was talking to and how mysterious she seemed. I was so deep in thought that I almost ran into Mr. Moon.

Mr. Moon was an old friend of my parents, the sweetest old man you could think of. "I'm so sorry, Mr. Moon," I said.

"It's okay," he replied. "Wow, I think

you've grown a couple inches since the last time I saw you."

"That could be possible," I said, and smiled. "My mom says I've been growing like a weed—whatever that means."

Mr. Moon chuckled. I looked at his gentle face, filled with wrinkles and kindness, then remembered why I was there.

"My sister Molly is putting on a Hawaiian luau party, and she needs a big plastic bowl. Do you have any?"

"I'm afraid most of those have sold out. That's probably because of the church potluck and fair around the corner."

"Oh," I said with a small sigh.

He started to rub his chin. "But we still might be able to find a solution." He led me down an aisle and stopped at a shelf where he picked up a blue plate. "Could you use this?"

I pulled out the crumpled-up piece of paper and opened it for him to see. "My sister wrote this list for me to remember what she needs me to get for her party, and she said for me to get only the stuff she put on the list. I don't think this would work."

"I see," he said as he put the plate back

on the shelf, "but it's the only thing we have."

I sighed. "Okay, that's fine."

He put his hand on my shoulder. "Hey, maybe there's some in the back."

I shrugged with a little bit of a worried frown, "Okay."

"Come on, Margaret, have hope," he said with his signature warm smile.

But when we got to the back of the store, we found that there was nothing. I could see that he looked disappointed that he couldn't help me. He was about to say something, but I spoke up before he could. "It's okay, Mr. Moon. I'm sure I'll find it somewhere."

Mr. Moon smiled and said, "Thank you for understanding."

I smiled back. "Thank you for your time." Then I waved at him and left.

On my way home, I was trying to think of the best way to break the news to Molly that I wasn't able to get the bowl she wanted, but while I was deep in thought, I almost ran into one of the neighbour kids named Andrew. Milliseconds before we collided, I swerved and fell into the ditch.

"Are you okay?" he called, quickly

running over to help me.

I wiped some dirt off my chin and grass off of my shirt and replied, "Yeah, I'm fine, I just got some dirt on my face."

"Okay," he said, smiling. "As long as you aren't hurt."

After he left, I slowly rolled my sleeve up and grabbed my right elbow. It had a big blue bruise along the edge. "Ouch," I whispered. I rolled my sleeve back down and picked up all the party things scattered across the sidewalk. I put them back into my bike basket. I really hoped Molly wouldn't be too stressed out that I was late.

When I got home, Molly came running out to greet me. At least I thought she was coming to greet me. "Did you get everything I asked for?" she said in a crazed voice. "I hope you did because the guests will be arriving soon, and I haven't even started to decorate!"

What a bossy eight-year-old, I thought a little grumpily to myself as I rubbed my elbow again. "Slow down, little tiger—I haven't even got off my bike yet."

"Well, then get off your bike! We can't waste any time!" Molly cried.

My face softened at her excitement, and I smiled. "Okay, okay, give me a sec." I gave her the basket and prayed that she'd forget about the bowl.

Molly frowned as she looked at the supplies. "Hmm . . . something is not right."

Please don't say the bowl, please don't say the bowl, I said in my head.

"You got purple and green jewelry boxes."

"And?"

"And I wanted purple and pink jewelry boxes."

"Well, you didn't exactly say what color you wanted."

"Margaret, you've known me for eight whole years. I think by now you would know that I would prefer pink rather than green."

"Molly! They didn't have pink," I blurted out.

"You should have told me that as soon as you got here," she said.

I shook my head, laughed, and gave her curly hair a tussle.

She looked in the bag again. "Um . . . not to be a problem, Margaret, but I did ask for a pretzel bowl."

"You did, and there were no bowls at the party store."

"Really? NO bowls?"

"No bowls," I repeated.

"That's very strange for a party store," she said, tapping her chin.

"There was a like a million people in there, and Mr. Moon said it was probably because there was a church potluck and fair around the corner from the party store. Sorry, Mol."

"I guess fairs are fun," she said quietly, but then a worried look crossed her face. "But I absolutely have to have a bowl for the pretzels!"

"Don't panic Molly, I'm sure we'll find a solution . . . actually, I already have one!" I pumped my fist in the air.

"What is it?" Molly asked with a hopeful smile and a renewed sparkle in her eye.

"You could use one of Mom's bowls."

She frowned. "But Mom's bowls aren't fancy."

"Well, what are you going to use then?"

"I don't know. I need your help."

I laughed an exasperated laugh. "But I

just suggested something and you're acting like Fancy Nancy."

"I just can't use Mom's bowls. They're just plain white. How is that fancy?"

"I don't know, maybe you could make it fancy."

"How do you make white bowls fancy?"

I smiled. "You'll have to figure that out on your own."

"Margaret! You can't just leave me here; I have guests that are going to be here in a few hours and I don't know what to do or where to start!" I stopped and looked back at poor Molly's face. She looked like she was about to cry, and I felt compassion.

"Okay, I'll help," I agreed.

A bright smile appeared on Molly's face, and she ran over to me and gave me a really tight hug. "Thank you, thank you, thank you!" she said cheerfully.

"Okay, too tight!" I said breathlessly.

"Oh, sorry!" She laughed and let go. Then, she put on her game face and said, "Follow me."

﹏

When we got to the bedroom, she pointed her two fingers out and motioned to her eyes, then to mine, like a spy. "This is what you are going to be doing first." She grabbed the piece of crumpled up paper from her pocket and showed it to me. "This is the plan for the party." She cleared her throat. "First I will entertain them with my fabulous hula dance. During that time you'll be making the caramel corn downstairs."

"First of all, do you even know how to hula dance, and second of all, about me making the caramel corn—"

"Don't worry," Molly said. "We have all the ingredients you'll need to make it."

"No, it's not that, it's just . . . I was kind of planning on reading during your party."

Molly slumped down on her bed. "But it won't be a fancy party without a waitress."

I sighed. "One batch of caramel corn, I guess."

"Thank you so much, Margaret!"

I smiled and bowed, and in a genuine way, said, "My pleasure."

"We need to get to work now," she said with a serious face.

Molly and I tidied up the house first,

which was Mom's idea, and then we began setting up all the party stuff. "Looks great," I said, turning in a full circle to take it all in once we were finished.

"It sure does," Molly said. Then, she gasped. "Look at the time, M.! They'll be here any minute now, and I haven't even got my party dress on yet!"

I smiled. "Calm down, Molly. Go get your dress on, and I'll watch the door."

"Thank you, Margaret!"

Three minutes passed before Molly came waltzing down to the front door. "Welcome to my—"

"They're not here yet, Molly," I said.

She opened her eyes wide. "They're not here yet?"

"Molly, you were only up there for a couple minutes," I said.

"Wait, Shh . . . "

"What?" I asked.

Molly ran up to the window. "I think I hear a car engine!"

"I really don't think that—"

"It's them! It's them!" Molly shouted.

"It's them? They're here?" Now I was the one that was sounding panicked.

"Yes!" Molly said. She quickly put a boa around my neck before opening the door.

A flock of little girls came racing in. "Hello, I'm Emma!" the first girl bubbled to my mom, who had stepped out into the entryway when she heard the doorbell. "Thank you dearly for inviting me to this splendid party here at my dear friend Molly's house," Emma said with a polite smile. She had a British accent, which made her sound very mature for an eight-year-old girl.

"You're very welcome, Emma. It's so nice to have you," Mom said warmly.

Then Molly pointed to a girl in the back. "This girl here," Molly said, pulling her to the front, "is Jenny."

"Hi," Jenny said a little shyly.

"I've seen you around the girls' school a few times," Mom said, shaking her hand.

I started to get bored of Molly introducing all her friends. I already knew most of them. I ran up to my bedroom and came back down. I sat on the couch and opened up my book to read it for a few minutes before starting the caramel corn, but I couldn't help overhearing Molly introducing her last friends.

"And you know Lola, Mom!" Molly said. She looked really happy with all her friends. Then, Molly pointed at a girl with a blonde, bouncy ponytail. "And now, last but not least, I give to you the one and only Brooklyn White!" Brooklyn laughed.

"Do I hear applause?" Molly shouted.

Brooklyn spoke up. "I think the applause should go to you, Molly. You did put on this amazing party."

Molly smiled. "Thanks, but the applause should probably go to my sister over there. She helped me with a lot of stuff."

I smiled and set my book down. "Thanks, sis."

"Aaaaaalright," Molly said, "let's get this luau started! Margaret, you know what to do."

I pointed back at her. "Yep."

Mom looked over her shoulder just in time to see me yawning. "Margaret, why don't you lie down on the couch for a little while, and I'll make the popcorn?"

I smiled, straightening Mom's red boa. "Thanks, Mom, but I can handle it."

"Margaret, you've worked very hard today. You need a break. Let me do it."

"Mom, it's okay. I can do it. You can go relax."

"No, Margaret, I feel like I've been relaxing all day, and you were working very hard with your sister. Please. Let me do it."

"Okay, Mom, you win. I'm tired of arguing." I laughed.

"Thank you for finally giving in. Now go lie down," Mom said with a smile.

"Thanks, Mom. Really."

Mom hugged me before getting up to start the caramel corn. "You're welcome."

Chapter 4 - Recapping

Okay, so a lot of things have happened in the past couple of days. First of all, I've been thinking a lot about school getting let out for summer break. I'm pretty excited about that, but I'm also really puzzled about one thing. We usually plan a lot for our trip, but Mom seems so relaxed about it. I hope we're still going to Hawaii.

I've also been thinking a lot about Miss Mary—Mom's high school friend. I know she's probably just an ordinary lady, but something about her just makes me wonder.

For starters, Mom invited her out to

lunch with us, but she said she was "busy." We haven't seen her very much. Mom tried inviting her to our house, and she said she'd love to, but she "couldn't make it that day." Something about her seems mysterious.

I just started folding a big basket of laundry. I don't really want to do it, but it'll give me some more time to think about things.

Molly's been pretending she's a detective, and she's on the same track as me where she thinks Miss Mary's not trustworthy. I've tried talking about it with Mom like she tells me to do when something is bothering me, but she just says that Miss Mary isn't up to anything and that she's a normal lady. I get it that Mom doesn't want to throw her friend under the bus, but she's being too protective of her. I seriously don't trust her . . . at all.

I don't know what to do about it, though. I mean, I'm just a kid. Maybe I'm just feeling this way because I read a lot of mystery novels, like Nancy Drew. I'm thinking of writing my own mystery novel someday.

I'm just going to try not to think about it.

Chapter 5 - Packing Day

"Pants, T-shirts, socks, and games. Molly." Mom put her hands on her hips. "This is my fourth time checking your suitcase."

"Is it good now?" Molly squealed.

"No!" Mom threw her hands in the air. "Molly Kate Mason, you forgot your underwear, swimsuit, shorts, and hair ties."

"You didn't check the top compartment."

"Yes, I di—ooh. Whoops," Mom said.

"It's okay, Mom." Molly smiled.

"Mom!" I yelled down the hall after overhearing this conversation.

"Shhh!" Mom ran out of the bedroom to meet me. "Your dad was up late last night and is still sleeping."

"Sorry," I whispered.

"It's okay. Come into the room." Mom led me into our room and sat me down on the bed. "Now, what is it?"

"I can't fit my Mermaid sunscreen or my deodorant into my suitcase."

"It's okay. I'll pack them in mine."

"Thanks, Mom," I said with a grin.

"You're welcome," Mom said. She was folding some extra socks for mine and Molly's suitcases. I was really happy because now I knew that we were definitely going on vacation. But were we still going to Hawaii?

"Now you'll LOVE this trip," Mom said with a wink.

"We're still going to Hawaii, right?" I asked.

"Wait!" Mom screeched. "Where did you hear that?"

"Molly told me," I shrugged.

Mom looked at Molly. "Wait, how'd you figure out where we were going?"

"Yeah, Molly," I said, "you said *Mom* told you."

"Um, Mom," Molly said, changing the subject. "Can I please dye my hair ocean blue?"

"No," Mom said without batting an eye.

"What?" she said. "I think I have a bunch of wax in my ears. Did you say no?"

"Yes, I did. Molly, how did you find out about the trip?"

"I was in your closet, and I found a bunch of brochures on Maui, Hawaii. I'm really sorry."

"We're going to Maui?" I squealed.

"Molly," Mom said in a stern but still calm voice.

"Uh-oh," she said. "I'm really sorry. I shouldn't've told M."

"No, it's not that. It's just that I don't appreciate that you were snooping in my closet."

Molly backed up. "Ooooh, about that—"

"Yes, about that. What were you doing in there?"

"I was trying to find interesting things in there," Molly said. "I'm *really* sorry."

"I forgive you, Molly, but no more digging in my closet

without permission."

"Yes, Mom," she said with genuine repentance.

"Mom?" I asked in my sweetest voice.

"Yes, sweetheart?"

"Uh, maybe I'm too old for that nickname now."

"No one's too old to be called sweetheart, sweetheart."

I sighed and grinned. "Do we get to ride in a big plane? You know, since we're going to Maui and all?"

"What do you think?" Mom asked me.

"Yes?"

Mom grinned. "You got it, girl."

I felt good inside. I loved my mother so much and couldn't imagine life without her.

Chapter 6 - No Sleep

"Lights out girls," Mom yelled from downstairs. "You have an early morning tomorrow."

"Already?" Molly yelled back.

"Yes, it's 8:30, and that's twenty minutes passed your bedtime."

"I hope we're able to sleep tonight. I'm really excited," I said to Molly, whose bed was now across from mine. Mom had taken my bed, clothes, and things to Molly's room a few days before so we could start sharing our room.

"Yeah, I am, too," Molly replied. "And look, I asked Mom if I could have one of the brochures, and she said yes."

"Wow, did you already look at it?" I asked.

"Just the first page. It looks really interesting. You want to look at it with me?"

"Sure, on the plane tomorrow."

"Why not now?"

"Mom said lights out."

"We did turn off our light. I have a flashlight with me."

"Well, I don't know, isn't that a bit, well, deceitful?"

Molly shrugged. "Fine. If you don't want to look at the hotel we're going to stay at, or the swimming pool at the hotel, or the ocean, or the tropical food, then . . ."

"Fine . . . just one page," I said, hesitating just for a minute.

It turned out that it wasn't "just one page." It was the whole brochure, plus the back of it, which wasn't important at all, just a bunch of locations where you can get more brochures of different tropical places. We spent a lot of time looking at the pictures, especially Molly, who was dying to get to the hotel and stretch out one of those comfy beach-style beds with light pink comforters that had seashells on them.

Before we knew it, it was nine o'clock, and Molly wanted to look at the brochure again. Of course, I immediately said no, but you know Molly. You know what that sneaky little girl did? She pulled out *another* brochure of the airline and airport, the same one we'd be at in only a few hours! And somehow, two minutes later, I was looking at the brochure, which was longer than the first one, and there were more pictures!

"Molly, where did you find this brochure?" I asked.

"It was in Mom's closet too."

"Well, it's already too late. We need to go to sleep."

"You don't want to look at it?"

"No! I don't want to see any—"

Molly interrupted me. "Please, M?"

"You heard Mom. We have an early morning tomorrow," I said. Then I did what any big sister would do. I rolled over quickly and pretended to fake snore until I was snoring for real.

When I woke Molly up the next morning, I heard that she hadn't fallen asleep until eleven.

Chapter 7 - Phone Call Goodbyes

"Margaret, please pass the toast," Mom said.

"Sure," I answered.

"Mom," Molly said tiredly. "I . . ." She paused to let out a huge yawn.

"Are you okay, Molly?" Dad asked from the head of the table. "You look tired, and you've been yawning a lot."

Molly looked at me, and I shook my head. "I'm fine," she said. "It's just . . . Mom said that we had to wake up early, and we did, but why did we? It's not like we had to catch a plane at six o'clock in the morning or anything."

"I didn't really want to have airport food for breakfast. If we wanted breakfast here, we would have to eat it early," Mom answered.

"Oh, that makes sense," Molly said.

"What time is it, Mom?" I asked.

"6:52," Mom answered promptly.

Molly quickly finished her eggs and jumped up out of her seat. "Can I call Lola and say goodbye?"

"It's pretty early, Molly. Maybe text her."

"Oh, no," Molly said. "Lola said she was going to get up early this morning so that we could give each other a call."

Mom sighed. "Okay, take my phone up to your room."

"Okay, thanks!" Molly ran up to our bedroom.

I asked Mom if I could text my friend Meg to say goodbye. Mom told me I could. I quickly grabbed my brand-new phone with its silver, sparkly cover with the words "I Love to Shine" on the back. It's a flip phone, and the only thing you can do on it is text and call. I covered the back with sparkly glue and took a sharpy to write the words on the back. He-he!

Anyway, back to Meg. Meg is one of my best friends. She goes to the same school as me, Jericho Elementary, and the only difference between us is that she's one year older than me. After a long text conversation, I tossed my phone into my backpack and threw it onto my shoulder.

"Mom! Guess what!" I said, storming down the stairs.

"What?" Mom gasped. "Wow, you scared me. I thought that someone was dying with that war cry."

"Sorry, Mom. Meg's getting a puppy!"

"That's exciting," Mom said while rinsing our breakfast bowls. "Does she know that we're getting a puppy, too?"

"Mom, she's practically family. Of course she knows."

Mom laughed. She looked me in the eye. "Can you tell Molly I said she has to come down?"

"Sure," I said, and then I started up the stairs.

Soon Molly and I were waving out our windows from the backseat to our neighbours as we drove down our street on our way to the airport.

Chapter 8 -
The "LONG" Drive

"Alright, enough texting goodbyes, M.," Mom said from the passenger's seat.

"Sure, just one sec. I'm almost done texting Brittany."

"Make it quick," Mom responded. I had been texting goodbyes the whole way now and everybody was tired of the background noise of me laughing and the *click click* of my thumbs. Everyone wanted to hear some music, so I quickly finished up my text and then shoved my phone into my pocket so that if any texts came, I wouldn't be distracted. I'd actually rather listen to Praise Radio instead of texting my friends, even though I love them dearly.

"Finally." Molly gave a sigh of relief.

Dad quickly turned on the Christian radio station. Finally, I thought, a bit of peace and quiet. I closed my eyes and leaned back in my seat. After only a few songs, though, Molly began begging to turn on a Princess album, and Mom was answering her, saying, "On the plane, you can listen to the Princess album, but not right now."

Then Dad was asking Mom how far from the airport we were and stressing out that we were going to miss the flight because the GPS was taking us the long way when really it was the fastest way. Mom was trying to explain that it was the quickest route, and then there was Molly in the background still asking for the Princess album, and all of us getting car sick. Let's just say that it felt like a very LONG drive, but we made it to the airport in plenty of time. Step by step, we made our way from the parking lot to the airport. There were a few stumbles along the way as we dragged our luggage along, but everything was going pretty fabulous . . .

. . . at least until we got into the airport.

Chapter 9 - Airport Incidents

"Well, here we are," Mom said.

"Now what?" Molly asked.

"Well, we have to go through security first, then we take it from there."

"Okay," Molly answered.

"Mom, I've only done this once before, and I don't remember correctly. Do Molly and I have to take our shoes off when we go through security?"

"Hmm." Mom started to think. "Well, remember, I've only done this a couple times before myself, and that might seem like a lot, but it doesn't feel like it because I haven't gone on a plane in many years." Mom sounded a little nervous.

"How old were you when you last went on one?" Molly asked.

"I was pregnant with you, Mol."

"Cool," Molly replied.

Mom smiled and seemed to relax a little as she gave Molly a side hug.

~

Finally, we made it to security. When it got to our turn, the woman standing behind the security desk pulled a bottle of blackberry energy juice out of the front zipper of the pouch of my backpack.

"You know you can't get past security with a drink, young lady," she said with a glare and a stern, monotone voice.

"Oh, uh, yeah, sorry, it's only my second time flying, and I was only three the last time I flew."

"You have the flu?" a little boy said behind me.

"No," the older girl beside him said. "She said she had the flu."

"No," I corrected them both. "I said this is the second time I *flew*."

"Seems like it," the girl mumbled.

I re-focused my thoughts back on the grumpy security woman behind the desk, who was now holding my blackberry drink over the garbage can. "Nooooo!" I said in what felt like a slow-motion voice. Then I heard my quick, frantic voice say, "You just can't throw away my energy boost. It's important."

She glared at me again, this time even harder. "You can get another one on the other side."

"You seem like a very nice young— " I didn't even get to finish my sentence before she grabbed my drink without hesitation and threw it in the trash with a loud thump.

I sniffled a bit but then threw my jacket and other carry-ons into the security bin. Mom patted my shoulder as she passed by me, and Molly patted my shoulder, too, though it felt like a slap. I was done with security and ready to move on.

Chapter 10 - Sub City &
the Masons

M olly and I were just coming out of the bathroom when we found Dad sitting on an airport bench. "When y'all were in the bathroom, there was an announcement. Our flight's been delayed a couple of hours," he said.

"So, does that mean we get to eat lunch here?" Molly asked.

Dad smiled. "You read my mind."

After a short walk through the airport, Molly stopped and breathed in deeply. "Ahh . . . you smell that?"

"What?" Mom asked as she set her

purse down on a cafe table.

"Sub City Sandwiches," Molly said in a dreamy voice.

"I don't smell anything," I said.

"Molly has pretty good hearing and smelling," Dad said.

"Sounds just like a dog," I joked.

"Hey!" Molly said, jabbing at my arm.

"Girls," Mom said. She looked at us with raised eyebrows and a half smile.

"Sorry, Mom," I said, glancing back at Molly.

Then Dad spoke up. "Speaking of Sub City, I'm feeling pretty hungry myself."

Mom smiled her warm smile that usually means yes. "I'm sure we can pick up some sandwiches. We don't really have anything else to do."

"Yay!" Molly made her excited, eight-year-old squeal that usually comes after something she considers a success.

"One problem," I said.

"What?" Molly asked.

"How do we know where to find Sub City?"

"Hmm . . . what about that map over there?" Dad pointed out a large map on a screen about twelve feet away.

"What about following my nose instead?" Molly inched over to Mom, who was now moving at a fairly quick pace toward the sign. "Mom, didn't you hear me? We can use my nose to get to Sub City. We don't need to walk all the way over there for a useless map."

I smirked. "But it's faster."

"I think my nose is faster." She nudged me, and I nudged her back. Soon we were at the map looking for directions.

"It says that there's two ways," Mom said, intensely studying it.

"That way looks the fastest." I pointed to a route through the airport that passed by a few gift shops, a salon, and a bookstore.

"Are you suggesting that it's the fastest way because there's a salon nearby, and as we walk by, you might just HAPPEN to need a hair trim, and you just HAPPEN to need your nails painted, and you'll say that you're willing to pay Mom back, but in your head, you're thinking she'll forget, and then you'll just HAPPEN to take advantage of your own mother?" Molly asked playfully.

"Why do you HAPPEN to keep saying

HAPPEN like that?" I asked with one hand on my hip.

"Molly, I don't think Margaret wants to take advantage of me. That's just the fastest way."

"Ooh, really?" Molly said, still sounding doubtful.

I stared at her for a moment. "Well, I guess we can go the longer way. Besides, we wouldn't have time for any of that."

Molly crossed her arms and then looked like she was thinking. "Well . . ." she said slowly. "In the end, it's really up to Mom and Dad." We all looked at each other and began to laugh.

"Margaret," Mom said, looking in my direction. "Can you take your backpack so I can carry my purse?"

"Sure, Mom."

"Can I help too?" Molly asked as she jogged behind us.

Mom looked over her shoulder at Molly, "I think it looks like all the jobs are taken for now, but maybe we can find something for you to do a little later."

Molly sighed. I felt bad for her, so I went over and playfully pushed her shoulder with mine. The corner of her mouth slid up a little in a crooked smile, but then she sighed again and slumped down.

"Molly," I said, "if you want, you can carry my backpack or jacket. I'm kinda getting hot."

She looked up at me, and her entire face lit up. "Really?" But then she went back to Molly the Suspicious and raised an eyebrow at me. "Wait. Are you just saying that to get out of your job?"

"No," I said. "I'm alarmed that you would take advantage of my kindness."

"I'm not trying to take advantage of your kindness; I just want to make sure. So, I'm going to take the jacket so you don't get out of your job."

Ugh.

Soon we were passing by the bookstore, and Molly—yes, Molly, the one who was scared that I was going to be tempted by a hair salon—stopped at the window. "Mom, can we please look at the books for a while? Please?"

I wanted to say something, but something inside me told me I shouldn't. *Just leave it alone, Margaret, or say something kind.*

I decided to just leave it alone. I didn't feel like saying anything kind at that moment, and I knew that was my own sin. I would have to pray about that later, but then I decided I should probably do that now, so I quietly said a quick prayer and then smiled.

Dad stepped into the conversation from just a few minutes ago. "You know what, Molly? I think we should get something to eat first and then maybe come back."

"Sounds like a plan," Mom said.

"Okay, I guess," Molly said.

Wow, that worked out.

Molly followed Mom and Dad all the way there without any more stops. I was shocked. I guess God had it under control after all.

When we got to Sub City, no one was waiting in line, which was good because our family usually takes a long time to order what we want. Mom grabbed Molly's hand and took her over to a little side menu to take a peek at the food options. I looked over at Dad, who was almost drooling over the smell of the restaurant's delicious food.

I grinned. "Dad, you should probably take a look at what they have before you go to the counter so you know what you're ordering."

"Are you kidding?" Dad said, "I know exactly what I'm going to order."

I raised an eyebrow at him. "Really, Dad?"

"No, no, for real. I . . . uh, well, don't tell your mom about this." Dad was now whispering. "But, uh, every time I have a lunch break when I go to work, I always go to Subs."

"Subs?" I questioned.

"Yeah, it's my code name for Sub City," he said with a silly smile and a wink.

"Mhmm," I said doubtingly. "What about the time you said that you were going to go to the salad bar two blocks away from your office? Was that the truth?"

"That? Ooh, I guess that time I did go to the salad place."

"Be careful with your statements, Dad. You're under oath," I said, solemnly placing my hand over my heart.

"Okay, we're ready," Mom said, walking back to us with Molly by her side.

"Are you actually ready?" I gave Molly and Mom an unbelieving look.

Mom chuckled. "Yes, we're actually ready. Umm, where's your dad?"

"Good one, Mom, but I don't fall for little jokes like that. Dad's right . . . wait, where is Dad?"

"Oh, heavens, sometimes he's just as mischievous as Molly—no offense Molly." Mom smiled, patting Molly's shoulder.

Molly gasped dramatically. "Offence taken . . . strongly."

"Sorry, Molly," I said as I looked around.

"Is that him up at the counter?" Molly pointed to someone wearing almost the same outfit as Dad, but when the guy turned around, it turned out to be only a teenager carrying a milkshake in one hand and a huge sub sandwich in the other.

"Nope," I said.

"I wasn't pointing to that guy," Molly argued, "I was pointing to the other guy at the counter over there." Sure enough, it was Dad.

Mom gave Molly a high five. "Good eye, kiddo."

We all made our way over to Dad, who I thought was ordering something he "wasn't allowed to," but he wasn't. It turned out he was so hungry he couldn't wait for food any longer, so he went to order ahead of us. After he was done, we all took turns ordering what we wanted, starting with Molly.

"May I please have a make-your-own sub?" she said.

The lady behind the counter smiled at Molly, "Sure, and what would ya like on that?"

"Hmm," Molly tapped on her chin. "Let's start with some mustard."

The woman poked at her screen and then looked up, "Okay."

"And bacon. You can never leave out bacon on a Sub City sandwich," Molly assured the woman.

"All right," she laughed, "What else?"

"Umm, cheddar, please."

"Sorry, one sec . . . Dan!" she called. A young man with dark brown, wavy hair, a hair net, plastic gloves, and an apron came from the back with some drinks in his hands.

"One moment, Hannah." He put the drinks down on the edge of the counter and yelled a name out. Then he came over to where we were standing.

"Sorry, Dan, I just got notified on the

computer that I'm needed to help clean up for a bit. Can you finish this order for me?"

"Sure thing."

"Thanks." She turned to us. "Would y'all excuse me?"

"Nice hair," Molly said to Dan when the lady had left.

He reached up and touched the top of his hair net. "Oh, thanks," he said, and then he finished up Molly's order with her.

"All right, next order."

I was next, and it was a very easy order. "I'll have a BLT, heavy on the B, light on the T, and simple on the L, please."

"Okay, anything else?"

"Yeah, I'll have a cherry soda, too."

"Awesome." He went to the mini fridge, grabbed my drink, and set it on the counter. "Okay, who's next?"

"Well, I'm the last one," Mom said. She went to the front.

"And what would you like, dude?" he said.

"Excuse me?" Mom said.

"Oh, sorry. Mrs. . . . um?"

"Mason, Mrs. Mason," Mom told him.

"Ahh," he said. "So, what would you like, Mrs. Mason?"

"A make-your-own style sandwich, please."

"What would you like on that?"

"Mayo, turkey, mustard, and a lot of olives, please."

Dad laughed. "She really loves her olives."

"Really?" the guy behind the counter asked excitedly. "Okay then, but the real question is, do you just love olives, or would you die for them?"

"She'd die for them," Dad answered.

"Hold on," Mom scolded Dad, "is that a trick question?"

"No," the guy said.

"She'd die for them," Dad repeated with a sly smile.

"I guess I would," Mom said, still trying to figure out if he was joking or not.

"Great!" He whipped his gloves back on and grabbed two handfuls of olives, almost using up the entire container. Molly and I stood there with our mouths almost dropping to the floor, both of us thinking the same thing: *what is he doing?!* When he was finished, he passed the flooded plastic plate of olives with a sub sandwich buried somewhere underneath to Mom, who looked like he had just given her a cold, dead fish. She thanked him politely and went to sit down.

We all laughed until our cheeks hurt at her olive sub, but then she ate it all up like a champ, after we prayed, of course.

Something caught my eye just then before I started to eat my sandwich. A tall woman with dark brown hair and a purple outfit. Was that Miss Mary? Why was she here? Something seemed very wrong. I didn't know anyone else noticed her until Molly quietly pointed her out to me.

Chapter 11 - Diction Check

When we were done at Sub City, we went to our gate and waited in some seats near the front. I turned my phone back on to check for any missed texts or calls. Ten texts and two missed calls, all from my two good friends, Meg Porch and Marshall Felix.

I scrolled through them:

Are you at the airport yet?

Have you eaten anything yet?

Tell me when you get to Maui!!!

My little sister (Natasha) wants to tell you something, can she call you?

"Oh no!" I said out loud.

"Are you okay, M.?" Dad asked worriedly.

"I'm fine," I said, "just missed a few important texts and two calls." (They weren't actually that important.)

"Me too," Dad said. "I had my phone turned off the whole time." Dad gestured toward his phone. Then he put it in his navy-blue backpack, tossed it in, and zipped up the orange zipper.

"Dad," I said, "why are you putting your phone away? I thought you were going to answer all of those phone calls and messages."

"Yeah, but it's too loud here. I'll put some headphones on once we're on the plane. Then I'll have a better working environment."

"Mom told me you can't text on the plane, Dad."

Dad rubbed his chin. "Oh, I forgot about that." He shrugged and grabbed his phone back out of his backpack.

I went over to sit by Molly and Mom so I wouldn't distract Dad from his work.

"What should I do on the plane?" Molly asked Mom in a whiny voice.

"You could color. I brought a coloring

book and pencils from home," Mom said.

"Or you could read?" I said.

"Read." Molly stared at me with a blank face, then started laughing, then went back to her blank face.

"I'm serious." I put my hands on my hips.

"Yeah, that's anti-fun. Coloring sounds great, Mom." Molly shook Mom's hand like she was making a deal with Mom. I rolled my eyes.

I looked directly at Molly even though I was talking to Mom. "When will my family enjoy the passion of reading?"

"Your dad likes to read." Mom smiled.

"Really?"

"Yep, every day, he reads lots of messages."

I slumped down, then said, "Molly, why did you want to stop at the bookstore if you aren't interested in reading?"

Molly seemed stumped for a minute but, like always, found an explanation. "There's always a good craft or art book at the bookstore."

We all heard a voice over the loudspeaker just then. A monotone voice boomed through the airport. "Flight 417 to Maui, Hawaii leaves shortly. If you are not already at your gate, you should be on your way."

"Eeeee," Molly squealed with excitement. "Can you guys believe we're going to be in Maui in only three and a half hours?"

"You're so accurate, Molly." I giggled.

Molly flipped her short, curly hair, "Thank you."

"Molly loves to be accurate," Mom said.

"Shouldn't you love school then?" I joked.

"I do, but one needs a break for some relaxation."

"Relaxation?"

"Yes, you heard me. If the word doesn't sound correct to you, you can look it up in the dictionary, or I can show you."

"Thanks, Molly. But—"

"We will begin with me showing you the pronunciation of the word."

"Molly, I appreciate the—"

"*Appreciate*. That's a good word, too, but for now, our focus is on the word *relaxation*. As I was saying, first I will write down the word with all of its pronunciation guides."

Molly started scribbling on her pink notebook with her purple pencil crayon. She showed me what she had written down. It was surprisingly neat.

'Relaxation'

After she showed me, she wrote some more words on the page:

Meaning: a. Relaxing in a certain place
b. Chilling out
c. Taking a break

I'm going to leave this up to God, I thought, although I felt like I wanted to say something sarcastic. I almost apologized, but that wouldn't make sense.

Then a peace came over me. I felt calm. I sometimes struggle with being annoyed or bossy, but at that moment, I felt like God was trying to teach me something about not getting worked up by Molly and having patience with her. She doesn't try to be annoying on purpose. She's just a little girl . . . my little sister.

Chapter 12 - Is That Who I Think It Is?

Finally, the loudspeaker turned back on, and a woman's voice began to give instructions. "We would like to start boarding passengers on the plane now. We will start with all the families with small children, and if anyone else needs extra help or time boarding, we would like to board them also."

Three families, including ours and one person in a wheelchair, all started to approach the gate agent. As Mom started to walk forward, Molly tugged back on her sleeve. "What are you doing, Mom?"

Mom turned back to look at Molly's worried face. "Molly, sweetheart, it's our turn to go on the plane."

"No," she corrected her earnestly, "the lady said she wants to board families with small children. We're not small children; we're teenagers!"

Mom laughed. "Well, Margaret's almost a teenager, but you're only eight."

"Does that mean I'm a small child?"

Mom laughed again. "You're a goofball, Molly, but seriously, we have to go right now."

Mom grabbed Molly's hand, and Dad took hold of mine. We somehow managed to get in line before a sports team made up of California teenagers. And they were all, "Dude." And we were all, "Sorry." After the apologies and the dudes, we quickly walked-ran to the plane.

When we got into the plane, Mom pointed to two rows across from each other. Mom got in with Molly, and Dad got in with me. Molly and I both sighed. "What's wrong, girls?" Mom asked.

"Margaret and me wanted to sit next to each other," Molly said.

"Maybe on the way back. We're all settled in now."

"But, Mom," I said from across the aisle. "It would be so much easier. Just think, you wouldn't have to tell her to stop biting her chapped lips all the time."

"And who else would do that?" Mom said.

"Me," I answered promptly.

Mom looked at Molly and gave her a thumbs up. Then Mom looked at Dad, and he shrugged. Mom sighed. "Fine, okay."

"Yessss," we both said. Molly punched her fists in the air.

Mom and Molly unbuckled and switched spots. We quickly got settled in.

⁓

The taxi drive out to the main airstrip where we were going to take off started right after Mom buckled in. It was a long taxi drive. I was enjoying the silence as I gazed out the window when Molly nudged me real hard in my ribs. "Ouch!" I squirmed around to look at Molly. "Why did ya do that?"

"Sorry," Molly said. She lowered her voice. "It's just, well . . . look over there."

"Where?" I started to frantically look all around me.

"No, over there, silly," she corrected.

"Oh, uh, what are we looking at?"

"That lady in the purple business skirt."

I saw her and gasped to myself. It was Miss Mary. Suddenly, I remembered seeing her in the airport while we were eating at Sub City.

"She looks like someone I've met before," Molly said, searching her memory.

I tried not to freak out. "Mom's high school friend?" I questioned.

"That's it!" Molly blurted out. "It's Miss Mary! Oh, Mom's going to be so excited!"

"So excited about what?" Mom said from the other row.

"It's your friend, Mom, Miss Mary!"

"Mary? Where is she?" Mom looked around a bit.

Molly giggled. "Right over—" She looked confused. I looked over to where Miss Mary had been sitting. She was gone. "Where did she go?"

"Molly, calm down. She must have gone to the bathroom, or maybe it was just someone who looked like her," Mom said soothingly.

"But Mom, she was actually here!"

Mom was back to looking at her magazine. "Nope, you can't have my magazine," she said. She must not have heard what Molly said.

Then Miss Mary came out of the bathroom. She looked around, then spotted Mom. Molly was glad and was going to say something, but Miss Mary quickly ducked into her seat and opened her phone. She started typing fast.

Molly frowned. "That's odd."

"It sure is," I said. My heart was still racing.

"Why would she just ignore Mom? She didn't even say hi!"

"Just let it go, Molly. She could have been in a rush or didn't want to bother Mom."

"But didn't you see the way she sat down that quick?"

"Well. Yeah."

"I dunno, something seems pretty fishy to me, M."

"Well, maybe we shouldn't worry about it. Meanwhile, I'm going to take a nap for the rest of the taxi drive." I put some earbuds in and fell asleep right away.

Molly stared at Miss Mary the whole taxi drive out. It took a little while to get there and get ready for take off, and I woke up right when the engine started. It was funny watching Molly fly back in her seat when the plane began to go up. She was so focused on spying on Miss Mary that she didn't even realize that the plane had started to take off. I looked over at Dad and Mom to see if they were doing okay, but they weren't. Dad was holding an air-sick bag, and Mom was holding two halves of the airplane magazine.

Oh no, I thought, this is not going well for anyone.

"Mom, did you rip the airline's magazine?" I asked.

Mom folded the ripped pieces and stuffed them under her chair.

"Umm . . . when the airplane took off, it just ripped."

"O . . . kay." Then I looked over at Molly. She had readjusted herself and was staring at Miss Mary again. "Molly, enough is enough."

"What?" was the innocent reply of my

little sister.

"You can't just stare at Mom's best friend the whole time we're on the plane."

"I'm not staring at Mom's best friend."

"Uh, you are. I can see you."

"Really? I thought Mom's best friend was Mrs. Taylor?"

Ugh, I thought. I felt like I was going to lose it. I was suspicious of Miss Mary, but I knew Mom didn't like us staring at people. "Okay, Mom's *good* friend," I corrected myself. "Just don't stare at her."

"Why can't I? I haven't heard any law saying I, or anybody else, isn't allowed to LOOK at someone."

"It's called staring, and it's rude."

"Well, who's saying I can't?"

"I am. And Mom would, too, if she knew." I leaned over to Mom, not to tell on Molly, but to ask if Molly could watch a movie. Otherwise, it was going to be a very long trip.

Chapter 13 - No Luggage

A busy flight attendant pushed a snack cart through the plane, stopping at each row to take orders. Finally, she passed our row, and Molly was very thankful because I think she was trying to find a reason to stop looking at Miss Mary. She had tried a few other things, like asking Mom if she could trade spots again and sit beside Mom because the lady in front of her had a very strong perfume on, and she was very uncomfortable with the odor.

Anyway, the flight attendant asked Mom and Dad what they wanted before she asked us, so Molly had to keep staring for a couple more minutes. I heard Mom ordering ice water and Dad ordering a cola, then Mom scolding him about it. My Mom doesn't like us to eat a lot of sugar or carbs. Mom's favourite verse in the Bible is Genesis 1:11: "And God said, 'Let the earth sprout vegetation, plants yielding seed, and fruit trees bearing fruit in which is their seed, each according to its own kind, on the earth.' And it was so."

Molly says she doesn't like that verse, but I always correct her. Truthfully, it's not quite my absolute favourite because it's used a lot in our house.

When the flight attendant was finished with Mom and Dad, she came over to Molly and me to take our orders.

"What . . . would . . . you . . . like?" She seemed pretty overwhelmed and panicked because she kept ending her words with a thud.

Molly was the first to speak up. "I'll have a bag of mini cookies and some apple juice."

"Okay, and your sister?"

"Umm . . . "

"Come on, Margaret," Molly urged, "the woman doesn't have all day."

"I'm just thinking," I said, and then looked up at the tired lady. "Sorry, I'll have a grape juice, please."

"Great," the attendant said. She walked over to her tray and started pouring juices into plastic cups, then went over to Miss Mary and gave her some tea. Molly watched carefully to see what kind of tea she was drinking, taking notes in her coloring book.

"Hmm, London Fog, I think."

Molly writes notes about different people or things to amuse us when she's bored, but this was getting tiring. I had decided that Miss Mary was just a regular woman. At least I hoped so.

The rest of the trip to Hawaii was a bunch of Mason stuff—I call it Mason stuff because that's our last name, and it usually means that we were "disturbing the peace." But when we arrived, something worse happened, and it started with a big Hawaiian guy coming over to us with a handful of leis.

He had a big cheerful smile as he put the flower necklaces over each of our necks. "It's like a boa," Molly said. When the guy left, Molly exclaimed, "Mom, I saw Miss Mary on the plane again!"

"Are you sure, Molly?"

"Yes," Molly said with a suspicious look in her eye.

I quickly cut in so Molly wouldn't say something about Miss Mary that might be rude in Mom's eyes. "Yeah, she was really busy and looked like she didn't want to interrupt you."

"Oh," Mom said disappointedly.

"Yeah." I started comforting Mom. "But hey, at least we know she's in Maui somewhere. Maybe we'll bump into her on our trip."

"I guess you're right." Mom smiled. "We better go get our luggage."

I didn't have a chance to stop Molly before her next words came out of her mouth.

"Mom, Miss Mary was acting really peculiar."

"Molly," I whispered in her ear.

"Peculiar?" Mom questioned.

I put a finger up to my neck and sliced it across as if to say, "don't even say it." But she did.

"Well, she looked really suspicious, and when she saw you, she ducked into her seat like she didn't want to talk to you or something."

I just about fainted. *You've done it now, little sister.*

Mom smiled an "oh, you are so sweet" kind of smile at Molly. "No, no. You see, Miss Mary is a very busy woman. She works for a clothing company and is trying to find a new job at the same time because the clothing store she works for is shutting down. I would say that's a big responsibility, wouldn't you?"

Whew. At least that's over, I thought. I patted Molly on the shoulder and said, "Well, I think we've all had our fun. Let's go get our luggage."

"I'm not faking it," Molly protested. "Something's up with Miss Mary, no matter who believes me. If you'll excuse me, I'm going to explore Hawaii now."

Molly marched off to the sliding door, and Mom went after her and spoke to her for a moment, then dragged her back to our group. "Okay," Mom said. "Molly and I have decided—"

Molly cut her off. "MOM has decided—"

"All right, *I* have decided that we will all see Hawaii together as a family."

"Great idea, Gwen—I mean Mom," Dad said quickly.

"Why thank you, Dad," Mom joked. "And you are right. It certainly is a great idea."

Mom and Dad exchanged amused looks. I knew that there was no actual decision. Mom would always have the same answer. She'd never let us out of her sight unless it was something like riding on our bikes to school.

"You guys are nuts," I said.

"We know," Dad kissed Mom on the cheek. "We're the nuttiest parents in Texas."

Mom chuckled. "We're in Maui, so I guess now we're the nuttiest parents in Hawaii."

"Mom, Dad," I said, "we should go get our luggage now. We don't want it to be stolen."

"I highly doubt that, Margaret," Molly said in a tone that sounded like one of our parents.

"Well, I highly doubt you're going to get to explore Hawaii today if we don't go right now," I said. I was starting to feel slightly annoyed again and tried to restrain myself.

Mom put her hands on her hips, "I highly doubt either of you girls will get to explore Maui today if you don't stop arguing."

"Yes, ma'am." Molly saluted Mom with her left hand.

"Uh, Molly, it's supposed to be your right hand," I corrected her.

"Don't blame me if I use my left hand; some humans are left-handed."

"Molly, you're not left-handed. I've seen you write with your right hand before."

"And where did you see me do that?"

Mom stepped in then. "Girls, we're wasting time."

"Sorry, Mom," we both said in unison. Though I felt like fighting this argument through, I took a deep breath and tried to give it over to God again.

"Step lively, folks," Molly called out to our family, who was about ten steps behind her. "We don't wanna waste time."

"Mom," I patted Mom's shoulder.

"What is it, M.?"

"Um, so . . ." I tried to sound calm, but it all just came bursting out. "Molly's being super annoying. Could she just stop pretending she's always in charge? She's not a parent!"

"Honey, Molly's a little girl. She doesn't think she's doing anything wrong. And she's really not."

"Well, she's sort of being noisy. And bossy," I added. *Take out "sort of,"* I thought to myself.

"Well, she's not sinning. That has to be our measure. If it's a sin, it's got to go. If it's not, we have to try to be a little more tolerant and understanding."

"I guess," I said. I still didn't think it was cute . . . at all. Mom put her arm around me.

"All right, troupe, let's go!" Molly directed. "Mom, Dad, you guys look for your bags, and Margaret and I will look for our stuff."

"Sounds good, hun," Dad said.

We looked for ten minutes, then twenty. Then it had been thirty minutes, and then thirty-five. We looked until everybody else from the plane had already left and the carousel belt had wound round and round, completely bare.

"Oh, dear," Mom said, tugging her short hair.

"I know that this might be a bad time, but I have to say I told you so," I said matter-of-factly.

Everybody looked at me.

"Not a good time, M.," Dad said with

an *I mean it* look.

"Yep, mhmm, just wanted to say that one thing, nothing else coming out of this girl, or should I say this mouth."

Molly and Mom groaned. "Does this mean we don't get to go to the beach today?" Molly whined.

"I don't know. I think we have to go to the baggage claim desk," Mom sighed. "The last time I went on a trip was when I was pregnant with Molly, and we had to go to the baggage claim desk because we thought our bags were stolen, but it was actually Margaret hiding them from us." Mom looked in my direction.

"I had only just turned four," I said, backing away with my hands in the air. Mom and Dad both ran their hands through their hair, sighed heavily, and then started off to find the baggage claim desk with Molly and me in tow.

Chapter 14 - The Baggage Desk

"**W**ell, let's find it while we can," Dad said.

"Find what, our luggage?" Molly asked.

"Isn't that what we've been trying to find the whole time?" I mumbled to myself.

Molly started writing down what we were going to do. She grabbed an orange gel pen out of her flowery pink and purple backpack, along with a sparkly notebook. I looked at what she had written after she was done with it:

Mission Plan: To find out where our luggage is, and have the person arrested who stole it!!!!

Of course, I showed Mom the book, and I was shocked at her response.

"Mom, look at this," I said.

"Aww, that's so cute. Did Molly do it?"

"Mom, aren't you going to like . . . scribble it out or something?"

Mom frowned. "No, she's just being eight," she said simply. She walked over to Dad and picked up her purse (which was the only thing that was left behind).

Then I saw Molly running over to Mom and asking her if she could have some lip gloss. Mom handed Molly her favourite sparkly pink lip gloss. I frowned and ran up to Mom after Molly walked away over to see Dad.

"Mom, I don't get it. Molly will wreck your lip gloss. How can you trust her?"

Mom took me aside for a moment. "I'm going to ask you a question, Margaret." She looked stern. "Do you think Molly would purposely try to wreck my favourite lip gloss?"

I shrugged, not knowing what else to do. Mom raised her eyebrows. "Okay, *why* would she wreck my lip gloss?"

I could see where Mom was going. "I don't know," I said with a sigh.

Mom looked me in the eyes. "Margaret, why are you being so hard on your sister?"

I couldn't answer.

"I'm going to let you think about this," Mom said, and then walked over to Dad and Molly.

I watched Molly pass Mom her lip gloss back. I knew what I had to do, but I just couldn't do it. I felt sad as I walked over to my family. I couldn't look at any of them.

-

Dad rallied everybody up. "Okay, family, on three, the Family Countdown, okay?"

"Okay," Molly and Mom said. I stayed silent. The Family Countdown is a thing that our family has been doing for . . . well, all of my life. We all put our hands in the middle and yell out a prayer request, a Bible verse, or a praise, and then we say, "The Masons."

"What should we do, a Bible verse or

a praise?" Dad asked everyone.

"Maybe a Bible verse?" Molly suggested.

"I think we should do a praise," I said.

Mom looked at me. I guess she was surprised that I was now speaking.

"Why?" Dad asked.

"Because there's no Bible verses about luggage being lost."

"Good point," Dad said, rubbing his smooth, shaved chin.

"Okay," Mom said. "But what praise would we do?"

"Everybody think," Molly said like a superior. She charged right into action. "Why not this? 'We lost our luggage, but Jesus will lead us!'"

"That's actually pretty good." I smiled. Even though I couldn't pull myself together for an apology, I could at least compliment Molly.

"Great job, Mol," Dad said.

"I think it's settled then." Mom grinned.

"All right, huddle up," Dad said, getting his game face on.

I stopped him. "Whoa, whoa, wait."

Dad put his arm around me. "What's up, M.?"

"Aren't we gonna do it privately?"

"Where else would we do it?"

"I don't know, maybe over in that corner?"

"You think that it's going to be quieter over there? Besides, don't you think it's important to make a public witness for Jesus?"

"Okay, Dad, you won," I said with a slight giggle. "And, yes, it is important."

Dad grinned. "Okay, everybody put a hand in the middle." Everybody happened to put their right hand in for some reason, and Dad instantly threw in a joke. "Looks like everyone chose the 'right' hand."

"Okay, Dad, you need to think of some new jokes, am I right?"

"Totally," Molly agreed.

Mom laughed. "Yes, he does."

"All right," Dad said with a laugh. "One . . . two . . . three!"

"We lost our luggage, but Jesus will lead us!"

It was kind of a disaster. Mom and Molly started way ahead, and Dad and I were singing it out, which wasn't bad, but Mom and Molly were saying it like a poem, and Dad and I were also off-key.

Dad scratched his head. "Well, it was

pretty good for the Masons."

"Dad," I said with a bit of a grin. "That was horrifying!"

"It kind of was." Mom sighed as she threw her purse back on her shoulder. Molly put her hands on her hips.

"I thought we agreed on poem style."

"No, you just showed us that way," I said with one firmly planted on my right hip.

"Well, I didn't think it would be that confusing," Molly burst out. I was about to say something else, but I thought for a second. Should I really keep this fight going, or should I try to end it calmly and trust God with my emotions? I decided to try to end it and be what the Bible calls a peacemaker.

"You're right, Molly," I said, even though it was hard to say.

Molly looked surprised. She pointed at her chest with her thumb. "Me? I'm right?"

"Yes. I'm sorry. It was kind of confusing for me. Will you forgive me?" I could hardly get the words out, but once I did, I felt better.

"Well . . . yeah, but I guess that I'm just so used to fighting it out that I didn't expect an apology so soon. I mean, we do fight and then forgive, but not halfway through the

fight. I guess it's wrong of me to think that. I'm the one who should be saying sorry."

"Molly, it's not just you that was wrong. It was me too."

"Well, I guess that's right. So will you forgive me?"

"Of course," I said.

"I forgive you, too," Molly said with a grin. I looked over at Mom, who was wiping her nose with a tissue and talking to Dad about how grown up we were. Molly and I hugged each other, made up a new secret sister handshake, and then went to get our luggage for real this time.

—

Finally, we reached the baggage claim desk and had to wait an hour for our turn. But something unexpected happened while we were in line,. It started with Molly looking around for interesting things that might catch her eye. Something sure caught it.

"This is taking for-ever, Mom. How much longer?" I complained.

"Oh, Margaret. Look at your eight-year-old sister standing in line as quiet as a mouse. Take an example from her. You might even be amused by what she's doing." Mom turned back around to talk to Dad. I sighed and looked at Molly, who was scanning around the crowd of people. (Probably to see if she could find who took our luggage.)

"Whatcha doing, sis?" I asked.

Molly turned around and looked me straight in my pupils.

"Looking for sneaky people that might have stolen our luggage," she said mysteriously.

I was right!

"Oh, nice . . . sooooo, want to rehearse our secret handshake?"

"Sorry, but I'm kind of busy right now."

"Oh, okay." I turned to grab my phone out of my backpack but then remembered our luggage wasn't there. I got up to turn around and heard a shriek from Molly. "Are you okay, Mol?"

"M., look." Molly pointed to a tall woman wearing purple heels. Her hair was piled up in a tight, tall bun, and she wore a silver ring on her pinky finger. "It's Miss Mary," Molly whispered.

"So?" I said, trying to be casual. "She was on the same plane as us. Maybe she was getting her luggage, and a phone call came in."

"Phone call?" Molly asked, perking up.

"Yeah, she's talking on the phone."

"Oh, let's try to listen!" Molly said.

"What? No, that's wrong."

"Don't worry, Margaret. We'll just see who she's talking to, then we'll go."

I didn't have a chance to stop Molly. She snuck through a bunch of people and caught up to Miss Mary.

"Molly," I said, trying to catch up with her. "Mol, stop."

"Shhhh, I'm trying to hear."

"Look, Mol, you've had your fun. Now let's get out of here." I pulled on Molly's pink t-shirt, but she tugged forward. "Molly! Are you insane?"

"Look, M, she's moving over there. Let's go!"

"Molly, she's going to see us," I hissed, trying to warn her.

"You're right! Hide behind that guy in the black overcoat."

"What if he moves?" I asked.

"Just do it, okay?"

"Fine, but if Mom catches us doing

this, you're going to explain what happened. Got me?" I said, giving her "the eye."

"Sure, whatever."

I was pretty sure she wasn't listening. Actually, I'm positive she wasn't listening.

"Did you hear me, Molly?"

"Listen!" Molly said.

"Listen to what? All I hear is the hustle and bustle of people rushing around."

"That's because you're not listening!"

I tried hard to hear so that Molly would be satisfied, but then I heard something that never left my mind. Well, that's a bit of an exaggeration. It did leave my mind, but that wasn't for a while.

Miss Mary kept pacing around, then finally she sighed and said, "Well, I can't find her either . . . I know . . . Yes, if you find her, contact me at once, and we will locate her together . . . No, I am not at the hotel yet . . . Yeah, when we find her, I'm going to make her pay . . . Okay, bye." Miss Mary tucked her phone into her purse, then went to a food court table and sat down.

Molly and I were shocked at this, especially me. After all, I was the one who didn't believe Molly in the beginning.

I grabbed Molly's sleeve, and this time she came along with me. I was kind of hoping Molly didn't hear all of what Miss Mary said because Molly might tell Mom or something . . . but she did, and she did.

"Mom, Mom!" Molly said, running up to Mom and Dad. They scooped up Molly and me in a huge hug and started talking over top of one another.

"Girls, where have you been?" Mom said. "Why didn't you tell us where you were going?"

Meanwhile, Dad said, "We thought you girls were lost! We were even thinking of calling security to find you two!"

"Mom, listen," Molly said.

"What is it, sweet pea?" Mom knelt next to Molly.

"We overheard Miss Mary talking on the phone, and—"

"Molly! Miss Mary may be here, but it's not good to listen to other people's conversations on the phone. Okay, hun?"

"Okay, Mom, but you won't even care if we listened to her conversation anymore after I tell you what we heard."

"I don't understand," Mom said as she

dug around in her purse.

"Just listen to this!" Molly said.

"Next!" The man at the desk called for Mom and Dad.

"Honey, you'll have to tell me later, okay?"

"But, Mom, I can be quick," Molly whined.

"Sorry, Mol, I have to go deal with our luggage situation right now. I'll be done in about fifteen to twenty minutes. Here's some snacks. Share them with your sister."

Mom handed Molly fruit snacks, a trail mix packet, and some M&M's. Molly sat there shocked for the first four minutes while I ate all the M&M's without even thinking. Then Dad came and sat down beside us.

"Looks like it's going to be a bit of a longer wait than we expected."

"So, we'll be here longer?" Molly asked.

"Yeah, I think a couple hours, maybe."

"What?" Molly and I said in unison.

"Yep, the day really goes by quickly."

"You can say that again," Molly said as she stuffed five fruit snacks in her mouth.

"Dad," I said.

"What's on your mind?"

"Uh, I was just wondering if you had

any gum in your backpack?"

"M., remember? No luggage."

"Right," I said with a sigh.

"Daddy, can I puh-lease wear a two-piece bathing suit to the beach?" Molly asked.

"No."

"Ugh!" Molly stomped her foot.

"Now, Molly," Dad began in his stern Dad voice. "I don't want any trouble on this trip. All right?"

"Yes, sir." Molly hung her head.

—

About twenty minutes later, Mom came rushing over to us. "Do you know what your suitcase looked like, Chris?" Mom asked.

"Yeah, it's brown with a black zipper."

"Great, thanks."

Ten seconds later, Mom came running back. "Sorry, I forgot if Molly's suitcase was purple or pink."

"It's neither," Molly said, popping a piece of chocolate from the trail mix in her mouth.

"What?" Mom sounded stressed.

"Yeah, it's violet with a scarlet red zipper."

I felt like throwing my head back and

roaring with laughter, but that wouldn't be very nice, so I didn't. Instead, I said, "Scarlet's a big word for an eight-year-old." I hoped she wouldn't take that offensively.

"I know. I know many words that other eight-year-old girls wouldn't know."

Whew!

"Of course you do. Back at home, you're the smartest eight-year-old on the block."

"I wouldn't say that because Lola and Natasha are on my block, too, and they're very smart. In fact, I would say all of us TOGETHER are the smartest eight-year-olds on the block."

"Yeah, I almost forgot about them." Molly raised an eyebrow at me. I giggled an "I'm so sorry" giggle, then turned around, grabbed a mint, and threw it in my mouth.

Chapter 15 -
The Mason Family

After another hour, Mom came over to sit down while security looked for something. Maybe it was fingerprints? By now Mom was really tired.

"After they're done checking the security cameras for our luggage, do you have to go back up there?" Dad asked.

So that's what it was. Not fingerprints. Whoops.

"Yeah, I think so," Mom replied.

"You've been up there for an hour, and they said it was going to be a couple of hours.

Why don't I go up there for the next hour?"

"That's sweet of you, Chris, but—"

"But she needs someone more responsible, like me," Molly said with a grin.

"Uh, no, Molly, that's kind of you and Dad for thinking of me, but I'm really okay."

"Aww, please, Mom. You know I'm responsible."

"Oh great," I mumbled.

"Oh, I know you're responsible, sweetheart, but Mommy's just gonna do it this time. Okay?"

"Okay. But Mom?"

"Mhmm?"

"Do you have any more candy left? Margaret ate them all."

Mom laughed. "That's sorta . . . funny."

"No, it's not," Molly said, sounding a bit more frantic. "I need candy."

"Sorry, Mol, but I just stopped at the vending machine along the way, and got a big bag of em'. I didn't know Margaret would eat all of them without sharing."

"It's okay, she's a growing girl," Molly said slyly.

"Ahem." I stood right next to her, glaring.

"What are you mad about, sweetie?"

Molly said.

"Oh, stop calling me that."

"What's going on, sweetie?" Mom asked.

Sweetie from Mom and Molly?

"Mom, would you and Molly both stop calling me that?" I said with a bit of a shouting tone.

"Oh, right. You're too old for that." Mom looked disappointed.

Then, Dad came over to sit with us. "How's my family doing?"

"Fine," Molly said.

"Just fine? I thought we were having an exciting and fun summer vacation together," Dad said. "What happened to all the joy?"

I sat there for a minute, thinking someone else would answer that question, but all I saw was my family staring at me.

Why were they staring at me?

I mean, yeah, I said I didn't want to be called sweetie but isn't that fair? Maybe I was being a bit cranky, and maybe I did need to change and put on a smile.

I didn't even have to think of what I was going to say to my family, and at the same time, I didn't really even know what I was going to say. But I felt like God was going to guide me with my words just like he did with Moses.

"I'm sorry," I said softly. "I need help being more gracious towards others and to be less grumpy at times when I'm feeling glum. Will you guys help me with that?" I asked, looking up at my family.

They all smiled at me, and Mom spoke for everyone, "Of course, dear, we all need help from each other."

—

There was only one more fight that evening, and it was about something silly. It started when the baggage claim people called Mom back up. Dad wanted to give Mom a rest, but Mom said that she had already had a big break when she came to sit with us while they were looking at the cameras for our suitcases. The little squabble between Mom and Dad only took ten seconds before Mom was up at the desk talking to the baggage claim people.

Dad, Molly, and I went back to the vending machine to get some more M&Ms, but before we even got back, we had eaten them all. Mom was still up at the counter, so we went to a little coffee shop/bakery in the airport and got some treats. We ate them there so if Mom came to sit down, she wouldn't see our treats. She'd get mad at us for eating too much sugar.

And there were a lot of treats. Two brownies to share, an iced caramel coffee for Dad, and three lemon lavender cookies. *A lot.*

After we ate it all and were cleaning up, I spotted purple heels in line. It was Miss Mary. Why was she staying at the airport for so long? I wanted to go over there and ask her what she was doing, but that would make me look dumb. So instead, I pulled Molly aside and pointed toward Miss Mary.

Molly gasped. "What shall we do?" she asked dramatically.

"I don't know, maybe just get out of here?"

"Dad's in the bathroom. We have some time. Let's go and listen to what she orders."

"What will that help us with?" I said.

"I don't know, just to see."

Apparently, Dad was just washing his hands so Mom wouldn't suspect that Dad took us for treats. He came out sooner than we had expected and scared us half to death.

"Hey, girls, what are y'all staring at?"

"Aaaahhh!" Molly and I screamed.

Dad looked around and scratched his head. "What's so scary?"

"What are you trying to do? Give us a heart attack?" I asked, still in shock.

"Uh . . . no," said Dad.

"Well, whatever that was, it was terrifying," Molly said with her hands on her pink cheeks.

"Sorry for scaring you girls, but we better get back to baggage claim, or your mom will wonder where we are."

"Okay, just one sec. Margaret and I have to use the bathroom."

Dad raised his eyebrows at us. "I was just in there ONE minute ago."

"Sorry, Dad," Molly fake apologized. "I guess we weren't thinking."

"Well, you better hurry up," Dad said as he moved back into the line. Probably for another treat.

"Great, that buys us some time," Molly said on our way to the bathroom. Molly can be a sneaky one at times—actually, most of the time.

"Time for what?" I asked although I had a pretty good idea what she was talking about.

"You know, silly." Sometimes Molly's too clever.

"Miss Mary. Right?"

"Right."

When we got into the bathroom, only one person was there. It was Miss Mary. I could tell by the purple heels. She was in one of the stalls. Molly and I jumped into the other one and onto the toilet seat. We over-heard a phone buzzing. Miss Mary grabbed the phone, and we heard her hang up.

Molly grabbed my hand and silently whispered something in my ear. She was so quiet that I couldn't hear her, but I was scared if I asked her to say it again, it would be too loud (I'm not a quiet whisperer at all). The good thing was that it just looked like Molly had told me something, so I wouldn't have to answer a question.

Molly looked at me again and did a thumbs-up. I shrugged and tried to show her in sign language that I didn't hear her when she whispered. It didn't really work out. Molly just frowned and shrugged.

I hit my forehead to tell her, "Just forget

it" but I hit it too loud. Molly freaked out and screamed without any noise coming out. She pushed me against the wall by accident.

We both freaked out, screamed, and pulled our hair out without any noise. Then we both heard Dad from the outside. "You two all right in there?"

We looked at each other, and Molly sliced her hands across her neck, signaling that we should not answer. NOW WHAT?

Chapter 16 - Masons on Bikes

Molly and I had no clue what to do, so we did something that was crazy but clever. We put our sweatshirts on backward, put our hoods over our faces, and then ran out of the stall and out of the bathroom. Of course, when we came out, Dad wanted to know why our shirts were on backward and our hoods were covering our faces. We didn't think about what our cover-up for Dad would be, but Molly can think of excuses faster than lightspeed.

"I know it looks very weird, but there

was a bad guy in there, and we didn't want him to see our faces."

Dad chuckled and kindly said, "Well, is that what you two were doing in there the whole time?"

"Yes," Molly answered matter-of-factly.

"Very sneaky and smart." Dad led us back to Mom, who was holding our luggage!

"Mom, you found it!" I yelped across the airport. Mom didn't want to draw attention, so she motioned for us to come over.

When we got there, she smiled at us and sniffed the air.

"So, what goodies did you get while I was at the baggage desk?"

Molly gasped. "How did you know?"

"My super cool nose and I managed to find out."

Dad tried to change the subject. "So, where was the luggage?"

"Where's the person who stole it?" Molly asked as she started looking around the airport.

"No one stole our luggage," Mom said.

"I knew it! Where—wait, what?"

"No one stole it. An elderly man accidentally picked Dad's suitcase up. He couldn't see very well and thought it was his."

"Okay," I said. "but what happened to the other ones?"

"They were lying on the floor behind a pillar," Mom answered.

"A-ha," Molly shouted with her index finger pointed up high in the air. "That proves that someone stole our luggage."

"No, that proves nothing," I said.

"Why?" Molly asked.

"Because if someone wanted to steal our luggage, they wouldn't just throw it on the floor and walk away," I pointed out.

"Good point," Molly said as she twisted her frizzy white-blonde hair with her finger.

"You should probably get the police on the investigation," I heard Dad say to Mom.

"I don't know what they could possibly do," Mom answered, a bit frazzled.

"We could solve this mystery by ourselves!" Molly suggested as she jumped around in circles.

Mom checked the time on her phone. "That would be fun, but it's getting late."

"Really? What time is it?" I asked.

"Six o'clock," Mom replied.

"Well, I'm not tired," Molly argued as

we walked out the airport slider doors.

"Well, you need a good sleep tonight because tomorrow we're going to the beach," Mom said.

"Cool, but I'm still not tired," Molly said without changing the tone of her voice.

"Okay, but you still have to go to bed," Dad added.

Molly groaned and shook her head like she had just lost something important and might never get it back.

Mom and Dad led us to some bicycles parked in a row. "These are what we're going to ride to the hotel on."

"Hold on, Mom. I know I'm supposed to respect and obey you, but I won't let you steal these bikes," Molly said firmly.

I wanted to hit my head and let my fingers slide down my face.

"Oh, honey, I'm not going to steal them. They're for rent. We paid for them."

"Oh," Molly said with a disappointed face. I guess Molly had just been confused. They didn't look like rental bikes. They were all different colors.

"Here, Molly, you can have the pink one." Mom handed Molly a brownish-pink bike with a straw basket and a purple bell.

Molly frowned. "This isn't pink. It's brown."

"There's kind of a pinky tone to it, and besides, that's the smallest bike," Mom said, pushing the bike toward Molly.

"Well, back home, I saw some teenagers riding smaller bikes than this one. Poor young adults. Probably the only bicycle they had."

"They choose to do it, Molly. They think it looks cool," I said with a blank face.

"Whatever, I guess I'll take the *brown* bike. You know, because I'm, like, really generous and loving," Molly said.

"Sheesh." I rolled my eyes.

"Hey, M.," Mom said, tapping my back.

"Yeah?"

"There's two bikes that are the same sizes. Do you want this one or this one?"

I looked at the two bikes. One was a bronze shade with a couple ancient looking orange floral designs on the side. The other was a pretty, sparkly, navy-blue color, with the word "Hawaii" in silver cursive letters.

"I like them both. Which one's your favourite, Mom?"

"That's very nice of you, sweetheart,

but you just go ahead and pick the one you like the best. I don't care which one I get."

"Thanks, Mom. I'll have the bronze one."

"Great," Mom said with a smile as she hopped on the blue bicycle.

"Where are we riding to?" Molly asked. She stuffed her video camera and mini scrapbook into the front basket that had little flowers sewn into the sides.

"To the hotel," Mom replied, sliding her phone into her shorts pocket.

"Aww, I thought we were going to go on an adventure bike ride, like all the way to Kaanapali beach or something," Molly said.

"How did you know about Kaanapali beach?" Mom asked. She crossed her arms the way Moms do when they think their kids are hiding something from them.

"I read it in the brochures you gave me to look at."

Mom softened her tone a bit. "Oh right, I forgot about those."

There was an awkward silence, but Dad straightened that out. "Well, it's getting dark. We better get going," he remarked.

"Right." Mom sighed.

"How are we going to get our luggage

to the hotel?" Molly asked. It was kind of a relief that Molly asked that question because I was dying to know how that was going to work, but I didn't want Molly to think that I didn't know.

Dad pointed to a baby bicycle carriage in the corner of the parking lot. "We asked if they could also park a baby carriage by our bikes so we could put our luggage in it."

"I guess that makes some sense," I said even though I still didn't get it.

"Okay, let's pile our luggage up in the cart."

Everybody grabbed a bag or two and helped get all our junk into the baby bike carriage. We were having a nice, smooth bike ride until Molly stopped to watch some hula dancers.

"Hey, guys! Look at those incredible dancers," she squeaked.

I was so excited when I heard her say that. I had always wanted to see hula dancers. I was sure Mom and Dad were also excited. The only other time they had been to Hawaii was on their honeymoon seventeen years ago. There was a bunch of chatter from everyone.

Me: "Where are they?"

Dad: "What kind of dancers are they?"

Mom: "Please tell me they're hula dancers."

Me: "Did someone say hula dancers?"

Mom: "I think I see them . . . Wait, oh no, that's just some little palm trees."

Then there was a CRASH, BOOM, THUD! Everybody was on the ground. I felt pain everywhere. I slowly lifted my head. Mom was already up and helping Molly to her feet. Dad was sitting in an awkward position by his bike.

"Mom," I said in a weak voice. "I think I broke my back."

Mom pranced over to the spot where I had fallen.

"Margaret, you'd be paralyzed if you broke your back, but I'm sure you're in a lot of pain."

Mom gently lifted my shirt to see my back. "There's gonna be a bruise, but I'm sure you'll be okay," she said with kindness in her eyes.

Molly wobbled over to Dad and asked him if he was okay.

Dad slowly got up. "I'm fine," he said.

Mom held out her hand to help me

up. I slowly lifted myself off the ground with Mom's help. I felt dizzy.

"Let's ride slowly and keep our eyes on the road," Dad said as he got back on his bike.

"Good idea," Molly said. "Ain't gonna make that mistake again."

We all laughed and slowly made our way to the hotel to take a nap.

Chapter 17 - Apelaoka Beach Resort

When I opened my eyes from my nap, I saw a bright light, and I thought for a split second that I had died and was on my way to the Promised Land—Heaven. The last thing I remembered was everyone falling to the ground. Then I remembered that we had gone for a nap.

When my eyes were fully open, I realized that it was just Molly's green flashlight given to her by Jenny Montez, our Spanish friend from church, on Molly's sixth birthday. What was Molly's flashlight doing in my face?

I sat up and rubbed my eyes to get the bright light out of my sight.

"She's awake," Molly yelped to my parents. They were in their hotel suite bedroom talking about something that I wasn't allowed to hear about until they figured out all the details.

"Don't bother your sister, Molly," Dad said with his booming voice. He crossed his big, hairy arms.

"Mmm," I grunted. I looked around from side to side. "Hey, we're in Hawaii."

"Yup, we're at Apelaoka Beach Resort."

"Apela what?"

"Apelaoka," Dad repeated.

"Ape—I can't say it."

"You'll get the hang of it after two fun weeks here."

I looked up to see a smiling Mom wearing a pink bathrobe with her hair up in a half-dry, messy bun.

"Hey, Mom," I said, rubbing my throbbing head.

"Hey, girly, you slept for a while there."

I blushed. Mom smiled at me. "Is your head okay? We didn't know if we should bring you two girls to the hospital to get checked up or not."

I shook my head. "I'm glad you didn't do that. How's everybody else?"

"Everyone's fine, just a few cuts." I looked over at Molly to see if she had gotten hurt, but her head was hanging down so I couldn't see.

"Molly, are you okay, honeybee?" She looked concerned.

"This is all my fault," Molly said sadly.

Dad and Mom looked at each other and then ran over to her. "No, no, honey, you just wanted to show us those hula dancers. You didn't know we were going to crash together," Mom said.

"Yeah, but if I had kept going, no one would have crashed."

"Look up at me, sweetheart. I was the one that wasn't paying attention to the road because I looked over at the hula dancers while I was supposed to be riding my bicycle. If I had stopped then, I wouldn't have run into you," Mom said.

I walked over to sit beside my family as Molly said, "But if I hadn't told you all to look, then you would have been in bed already having a nice calm sleep with no scrapes or bruises."

The back-and-forth argument about who caused the crash was kind of funny, but I forced myself not to laugh.

"You have to stop blaming yourself, Mol," Dad said as he rubbed Molly's back.

"Yeah, hun, we love you so much, and we know you didn't want this to happen. Right?" Mom asked with a kind face.

"No," Molly sniffled.

"And you didn't know we were going to fall, right?" Mom said and squeezed Molly's hand.

"No," Molly said with heavy shoulders.

"Then it wasn't your fault at all, see?"

"Why?"

"Well, you didn't mean to do any of this, so it wasn't your fault."

"Okay, I think I get what you're trying to say now."

Mom smiled and scooped Molly up in a huge hug. "Get in here, Chris and Margaret," Mom said with a grin. So we did and had a big Mason family group hug.

"I can't wait to spend these weeks with my family at Apelaoka Resort," I said with a smile. My eyes brightened. "Hey, I said it!"

"What did I tell you?" Dad said with a grin on his face.

"Now," Mom said after the big family hug. "I am going to get my PJs on."

"Me too," I said.

"I'll help you with your PJs, pumpkin." Dad smiled as he took Molly's hand and dragged her to her room.

—

When Molly came out of the room with Dad and Mom, she was squealing like a mouse. "What's up?" I asked Molly.

"We're going to watch an episode of *Kitty Cat's Adventure!*"

"Cool," I murmured.

"Here, M., take my arm. We're going to change that bandage and get you some comfy clothes to wear," Mom said.

Then, once I was all bandaged and changed, we watched Kitty Cat's Adventure. Not exactly my choice—but it was great to be with my family after a long day.

Chapter 18 - Family Issues

After the show, we were all pretty tired. It was nine o'clock, and everyone was pooped out.

"Time for bed, ya sleepy heads," Dad said as he attacked Molly with overwhelming tickles. I don't know how that girl can handle that many tickles. I mean, like, whenever someone even says the word "tickle," I run up to my bedroom and hide under my multi-colored polka-dot blankets and have a panic attack or something.

"Hey, Margaret, you want a little tickle?" Dad said.

"Aaaakkk!" I screamed.

I ran into our big hotel room and hid under the sea-green covers. "Hey, M., you in here?"

"No!" I shouted from under the covers without even thinking.

Dad did a slow laugh and then carefully pulled the covers back. "Sorry if I scared you, sweetheart. I was just trying to have some fun."

"It's okay, Dad. I just have a fear of tickles, and apparently when I hear the word, I get super hyper and overwhelmed."

"You're such a comedian, Margaret Sierra Mason," Dad said with a chuckle.

"I'm hoping you meant that as a compliment," I said with a squinty eye.

Dad and I shared a calm, tired laugh. Then we heard Mom shout from another room. "Chris, come here, now! I need to talk to you about something."

Dad jumped out of his seat and ran into the warm hotel room. When Mom saw Dad rush in, she instantly started to flail her arms around rapidly and chatter off words.

"Whoa, slow down, Gwen, the kids are standing right here."

Mom completely stopped when she

saw Molly and me staring at her. "Umm, girls, it's time to get ready for bed."

"We're already geared up," Molly said. She started to take out her two frizzy buns held up in her hair by two sparkly elastic bands.

"Did you brush your teeth?" Dad asked, looking at our mouths.

Molly opened her mouth to say something but then closed it. "Well . . . can't we do that after? Please?"

"Nope," Mom said with a grunt.

Molly grunted back and stomped her way to the bathroom. I pretended like I was going to go to the room too, but really, I stayed just behind the wall so I could hear what they were saying. But all I could hear were mumbled whispers.

—

When I woke up in the morning, I was desperate to understand what Mom and Dad were whispering about the other night. I sprung out of bed and ran to the bathroom to get dressed.

When I came out, I saw Molly right outside the door, lying down on her back.

"Molly, are you okay?"

"Wha?" Molly said like she had just seen a monster with twelve eyeballs. She hopped up off the ground and frantically looked around back and forth.

"What happened, Mol?" I asked.

Molly looked over at me. "Margaret?"

"Uh, yes?" I said as I tapped my foot on the carpeted ground.

"Well," Molly said, "the last thing I remember was that I was getting out of bed to wash my face, and then I saw a ladybug on the ground and sat down with it. Maybe I fell asleep while I was playing around with the cute little thing."

"Nice. Now can you move out of the way so I can get to the washroom?"

"Oh, right, sorry," she said, hopping up off the ground.

I grabbed a bundle of clothes I had dropped when I saw Molly on the ground, then rushed to the slider door, opened it, and ran in. I grabbed a brush off the creamy, marbled counter, swished it under the warm tap water, and then started combing it through my wavy, dark blonde curls.

When I was finished getting dressed and brushing my teeth, I ran into the suite's dining room and right up to Mom. "Mom, what were you talking about to Dad yesterday evening?"

"Is Molly still sleeping?" Mom asked.

"No, but I could try to get her to fall asleep," I replied.

"No, I want her to hear this, too," Mom said.

"I'll get her then," I said and ran out of the room.

"Okay, but don't rush her," Mom called after me.

I did. "Molly, Molly!"

"Shhh. I'm in the bathroom."

"Hurry up. Mom and Dad are waiting for you so they can tell us something."

"Waiting for me?" Molly sounded surprised and happy at the same time.

"Yes, you—now move it and hurry up."

"Margaret, remember what I told you," Mom called from the couch by the TV.

"Right," I called back.

"Hey, M., tell Mom that I'm coming.'"

Gulp. "But Molly, then they'll think that I was rushing you."

Silence. Then I saw a pink cheese ball somersault out of the bathroom. "Whoa," I said as I jumped back.

"I didn't mean to flip out like that," Molly said. "It's just my big bag of beauty fell off the counter and onto my back right when the door opened, and it all fell out."

"Big bag of beauty?" I asked, quite confused.

"Yeah," Molly said as she adjusted her fluffy pink bathrobe. "It's a bag with beauuuutiful things in it that make me beauuuutiful."

"What kinds of beauuuutiful things?"

"You know, lip gloss, eyeshadow, hair ribbons, and—"

"Wait, you packed eyeshadow? You're not allowed to wear eyeshadow!"

"Well, you aren't either."

"Uh, ahem, I'm eleven, almost twelve. And Mom never bought you eyeshadow," I said with a scowl.

"Why are we even having this conversation? I didn't bring my eyeshadow."

"Oh," I said, relieved.

"I brought yours with me because you never wear it," Molly added.

My eyes went big again.

"What?" Molly questioned. "Mom doesn't even really let you wear it."

"Well, no, not often, but she would never let you wear any eyeshadow until you're my age, anyway."

The eyeshadow had been a present from my Aunty Rose a while back. Mom hadn't liked the idea of me wearing make-up so early, so I didn't usually wear it. But Molly was definitely not allowed to wear it.

"Girls! Are you in here?" It was Mom. "What's going on?" Mom asked once she was in the room.

"Molly packed eyeshadow," I said, pointing in Molly's direction.

Mom's eyes got big. "Molly, you did?"

Before Molly spoke, I added, "And she packed *my* eyeshadow."

"M., let your sister answer my question." She turned back towards Molly.

"Well yeah, it's just . . . I was trying to impress Venessa—that super mean girl from Margaret's class—because she was teasing me before the trip. She said I didn't wear anything fashionable and should take a fashion class before going."

"I bet that's not even a thing," I said. Steam rose inside me as I thought about Venessa—she was super annoying.

"Probably not, but the point is, I was trying to be cool and impress her and for some crazy reason, I said that I had eyeshadow. For proof, I snuck into Margaret's room and grabbed the eyeshadow, took it outside, and gathered all of her friends with me. Then I showed her the stuff. She said I wasn't telling the truth and it was yours, Mom. So then I told another lie—or maybe it was a white lie."

"What?" I asked.

"I said that it wasn't yours, Mom, which it wasn't, but then I said again that it was mine. I even packed it in my suitcase and showed them all. It was a couple hours after you had checked my suitcase," Molly said.

"Mol," Mom said as she cuddled her into a hug. "Why did you do that?"

"I don't know. Sorry," Molly said.

I was madder at Venessa right now than I ever was at Molly. There's a reason people call her Venessa Flytrap.

"You know, there's a verse in the Bible," Mom said. "James 3:14. It says, 'But if you have bitter jealousy and selfish ambition in your heart, do not boast and be false to the truth.'" Molly sighed and hung her head. Mom looked at her kindly. "Molly, I don't want you to boast about things you don't have. Especially when someone's bullying you. You shouldn't want to impress people who are unkind to you, or anyone else for that matter."

"You're right, Mom," Molly said with another sigh.

Mom kissed the top of Molly's head, then turned to me. "Margaret, I hope you've learned a lesson, too, dear."

"Yeah, well, I guess I have. But I still think that Venessa's in the wrong."

"Well, of course," Mom said, pulling me closer to her and Molly. "But I just want to teach you two girls what to do next time something like this happens to either of you."

I thought about it and knew that my mom was right. "I love y'all so much," Mom said in an extra strong Texan accent.

After we hugged each other, Mom checked her shiny bronze watch. "Oh, my goodness, I need to talk to you girls about something before we get moving on, so hurry up, Molly, and get dressed."

"Okay." Molly put on her detective mode and started jumping around the room doing James Bond stunts.

"Ya squirt," I said teasingly as I nudged her shoulder. "You heard Mom. Get moving."

"Fine," Molly said as she started taking her bathrobe off.

"Not in here, Mol," I said, shoving her towards the bathroom.

"Right. I have to do it secretly." She instantly struck back in super-secret agent mode. Mom and I chuckled and left the room.

—

In a few minutes, Molly entered the living room wearing a yellow T-shirt with daisies on the front. On the back, it had yellow block letters that said "I'm Daisy of Daisies." It's supposed to mean in normal language, "I'm dizzy of daisies."

I know. It makes no sense. Whatever.

"That's probably the best shirt to wear today that will keep you cool enough."

"I know. I do look pretty cool." Molly said, wagging her eyebrows up and down at Mom and Dad. They shared a parent laugh.

I was about to burst. I really wanted to know what Mom was going to tell us!

Chapter 19 - Does It Make Sense Now?

M om got up off the couch. "Well, we should probably go get some fresh air before it gets too late in the day," she said with a sneaky smile, as though she was hiding a secret or surprise.

"But, Mom, I thought you had something to tell us," I said with panic. My mouth and throat were completely dry.

"Oh, right. Sit down, girls; there's something we need to talk about before we get out of this stuffy hotel for a nice walk somewhere."

"I think it's a lovely hotel," Molly said, smiling as she took a big breath of air and then coughed. That made me want to laugh.

Mom chuckled. "It is a nice hotel, but don't you wanna get out and go for a bike ride or something?"

"No."

Mom looked surprised but then folded her hands in her lap contently and pressed her lips together. "Well then, I suppose you wouldn't like to go to the hula dancing show this afternoon at one p.m., would you?"

So that's why Mom looked so sneaky.

Molly didn't really have an answer to this, so as the loving big sister I am, I flew right in to save her. "Oh no, she wouldn't miss that for the world."

"Actually—"

"Ba-ba-ba-bap," I said, cutting Molly off.

"Ba-ba what?" Molly asked with her arms folded.

"Doesn't matter. Go right on, Mama." Why did I say that? I thought, feeling kind of embarrassed.

I cleared my throat, and Mom continued talking. "So, as I was saying, the security at the airport found something that might help us with this luggage mystery." Molly leaned in closer, and Mom pushed her stylish strawberry-blonde hair aside. "So, it seems that there was this guy in the airport that had some drugs with him. He didn't just want to carry them around—otherwise, people could see him with the drugs and call security on him. So, when he saw our suitcases, he thought he could hide them there."

"So, what happened?" Molly asked with wide eyes.

"Listen to find out," Mom said, trying to continue. Molly pretended to lock her lips with an imaginary key and then threw the fake key away.

"He grabbed our suitcases and stuffed all the drugs in there. But he didn't need all of our luggage, so he threw you girls' suitcases down by that pillar where we found them."

"What happened to yours, Mom? Don't you have your suitcase too?" I asked.

"Well, he had my suitcase, and he thought everything was going fine until he came to security."

Molly frowned and held her index finger in front of Mom's face. "Wait, wait, wait.

I thought that he already came through security."

"Oh no, he's from Hawaii. He was hoping to bring the drugs somewhere else, although they don't know where yet. Anyway, he was going to bring them somewhere to try to sell them."

"Sell them?" Molly asked. Sometimes she struggles with listening.

"Just listen, sis," I said as I nudged Molly's forearm.

Mom smiled and kept talking. "So, you see, he didn't really have a plan to get through security."

Molly punched her fist in the air. "So, this is where he gets caught, huh?"

I rolled my eyes. "Molly, will you just pay attention, please?"

"That's easy for you to say," Molly whined.

"What do you mean?"

"I mean, you don't have so much pressure on yourself."

"What do you mean by that? And what does that have to do with paying attention to what Mom's telling us?"

Molly was speechless. Clearly, she

didn't have a response to this one.

"As you were saying, Mom," Molly responded sheepishly. That was pretty much all she could say at a time like that.

"Well, he's at security at this point, and everything was going perfect until it was his turn. He didn't know what he was going to do, so instead of thinking it through, he quickly ran through the security and even knocked down a desk with everyone's backpacks and bags on it."

Molly gasped. "Then what happened? Then what happened?"

"Well, boy, was he in trouble now. After the desk fell over, it blocked the way out. For him, it was perfect. All he had to do was run out. They had to jump over the knocked-over security desk and run after him."

"An airport chase! Why didn't we see it happen?"

"Well, we were close to the back of the plane, so it took a little while for us to get to the luggage belt. It had probably already happened."

"Okay, I see, I see," Molly replied with thoughtfulness.

"So, this guy's running, and the security is chasing him. He's pretty scared right now, but the security can't catch him, so they call some more security to help them try to catch him."

"Did they catch him?" That was asked by Molly—of course.

We both stared at Molly.

"Sorry," she said with red cheeks.

"It's okay. You just have to listen and not ask so many questions," Mom replied with a grin.

"Gotcha," Molly shot back.

"So, yes, they did finally catch him after the other officers from the department of security came."

"Wow, the security officers must be pretty slow," I said as I got up and grabbed a banana out of the small bowl of fruit on the counter."

"Don't be rude, M.," Dad said as he came out of the other hotel room where he had been changing into a pair of shorts.

"Well, they couldn't be too slow if they caught him," Molly suggested, trying to impress Dad. "They probably surrounded him."

"Actually, they did," Mom said.

"Told ya," Molly said with a little wink

that turned out to be more of a blink. I giggled. Molly rolled her eyes. Mom got up and grabbed her sunglasses off a wooden shelf in the room.

"Alrighty, let's get a-movin'."

Molly got off the small purple stool she had been sitting on and grabbed her jean jacket off the coat rack.

"How did you sneak that into your suitcase? I thought I checked it," Mom said with a frown.

"You did. And I didn't have the jean jacket in my suitcase."

"Where did you pack it then?" Mom asked as she took it off of Molly.

"I didn't pack it. I wore it the day we left."

"Ya sneaky little meatball," Dad said as he picked her up and plunged her back down on the couch. Then the tickles came.

Chapter 20 - Hula, Kahuna, and Me

When we finally managed to make it outside, it was 12:32 and the hula dancing show was at one.

"We're gonna be late, guys. Hurry up," Molly said, shouting orders out to the family.

"Okay, Mol, we get it. But if you keep telling us what to do, we'll never make it to the show in time," I said with my arms crossed.

"Give her a break, hun. She's only eight," Mom said instructively.

"Excuse me, but I'm not only eight, I *am* eight." When she said eight, it was in a

dramatic sort of way that comes out natural-
ly for Molly.

"Yes, sweetie, you're eight," Mom said,
not really paying attention to what Molly was
trying to say and what answer she wanted.

We kept walking for a little while but
then stopped and realized that we would
never make it in time if we walked the whole
way. We decided to grab the bikes Dad had
rented.

"What time is it, Mom?" I asked as I
hopped onto my bike with a quick prayer
not to crash again.

Mom grabbed her sparkly red phone
out of her jeans pocket but stopped in her
tracks. "Can't you just take a look at your
phone?" she said, giving me Mom Eyebrows.
"You know, that's one of the reasons we got
that phone for you. So you wouldn't be asking me what time it was so much?"

"Really, Mom? That's the reason you
got me the phone?" I asked, knowing that it
was not the main reason.

"I didn't say that was the only reason, but
. . . since you asked. It's, umm, twelve-forty."

"Thanks for that quick notification, Mom."

"Don't be rude," Mom said, wiggling

her finger in my face. Everyone jumped onto their bicycles and zoomed off.

—

We passed by a couple of small beaches and a few little outdoor food markets on our way to the show. Molly was so distracted by everything around her that she was hardly paying attention to where she was going. I even think she'd pay more attention with a blindfold on.

Molly gasped. "Margaret, look at that surfer! That's a huge wave he's on there. Oooh, and look at that ice cream shop. I vote to go there after the show! Look, Look! There's white sand on that beach! Amazing!" Molly was swerving all over the place.

"Hey, Mol, stay on the path," Dad called. Molly lifted her hand off the handle and gave Dad a thumbs-up. "Molly Kate Mason, I mean it. Pay attention. We are not going to crash again."

Uh-oh. Molly's middle name. Dad only uses it when Molly's doing something dangerous and he doesn't want her to get hurt, but at the same time, he sounds stern.

"Yes, Daddy," Molly called out to him.

"Hey, Mom," I called. "I think I can see the show starting."

"Yeah, me too. Let's go," Mom said, picking up her pace a bit.

"Yay! We're here," Molly cried when we arrived.

"Yahoo," Mom said, parking her bike in a small corner near the area. We started walking toward the stage. A Hawaiian man stood in the corner of one of the stands, and when he saw us, he came over to greet us.

"Hello, I'm Kahuna. May I help you?"

"Yes, we're here to see the hula dancing show," Mom smiled as she spoke.

"Show?" The man looked confused.

"Yes, I heard that there was supposed to be a show today at one. I even double-checked with the guy at the hotel we're staying at. He said it was at one o'clock today."

"You are correct. It was supposed to be today, but our lead dancer sprained her ankle and can't perform for a few days."

"Oh, no," Mom said compassionately.

"I know, it's sad. Tina was really looking forward to doing it today, too."

"Who's Tina?" Molly asked curiously.

"My apologies. Tina is my younger sister; she is the one who cannot dance."

Molly tugged on Mom's T-shirt. "Does this mean we can't watch the show today?"

"I'm afraid so," Mom responded.

"Oh," Molly said disappointedly as she hung her head low. I think I even saw a teardrop slip down her freckled cheek and onto her shirt.

The man saw that Molly was let down by this, and he knelt beside her. "Would you like to meet a couple of the dancers?" he asked her.

"Would I ever!" Molly said in an excited sniffle.

Kahuna then stood up and grinned. "This way, please."

He led us up onto the platform that all the dancers were standing on talking. A bunch of smiling Hawaiian teens stood in a perfect row on the little brown stage. The girls were dressed in beige grass skirts and little coconut bikinis. Not the most appropriate choice of clothing, but I guess that was their costume. They also had pink flower boas on. The boys wore green grass skirts and multi-colored flower boas.

"Tina, my sister—she used to wear a flower crown when she led the dance." Kahuna hung his head.

"I'm very sorry about your sister. When do you think she'll be able to perform the hula with these kids?" Dad asked to lift the mood.

"Don't worry, guys," Molly said, addressing the dancers. "My dad only says kids because he's old and thinks that Margaret and I are his babies, and he thinks teenagers are kids. And you know what he calls babies?"

"That's probably a good conversation for later," I said to Molly as I stepped on her foot. Dad went all red and stepped back off the stage.

Kahuna laughed. "It's okay. I have a daughter myself. You don't wanna know what she says out in public sometimes."

Mom pulled Dad back on the small stage. "Yes, I'm sure Chris and I know how that feels sometimes. Right, Chris?"

"Who's Chris?" Kahuna asked.

"Oh, my bad. Chris is my husband," Mom said, gesturing to Dad.

"Nice to meet you, Chris." Kahuna held out his hand to Dad's.

"And you must be Molly and Margaret," Kahuna said, looking down at our forever sister bracelets with our names on them. We wear them all the time.

Molly smiled. "You got that right!"

"Excuse me one moment, girls, but your dad was asking me when they will be able to perform." Dad smiled and winked at us. "As you were saying, sir. I'm pretty sure that they will be able to perform next week."

"Oh, that's great," Dad said with a smile.

"Now I can introduce you all to our dancers here," Kahuna said with a big grin.

"Yay," Molly screeched.

Kahuna pointed to the first dancer—a girl. "This is Demi," he said.

"Hello." She was so pretty with her olive-colored skin and black hair hanging down by her shoulders.

"Demi is the substitute teacher," Kahuna explained. "When I am sick or unable to come, she is my cover."

"I didn't know you taught them," Mom said, looking like she was ready for a conversation.

"Yes, I know the dance very well. My Grammy taught it to me when I was six years old. When my mother was in the hospital having Tina, I was very nervous, so my Grammy taught me the dance to pass the time."

"How sweet," Mom said with a loving smile.

"This is Keanu, a very skilled hula dancer." To me, he looked kind of young. About fifteen, maybe? I decided to ask him.

"Umm, excuse me, how old are you?"

The boy started saying a bunch of words in a language I didn't know. "He does not speak English," Kahuna said. "Only Polynesian. But he does want to learn."

"Okay, but what's Polynesian?" I asked.

"It is the language we speak here."

"But I thought you spoke Hawaiian?" I said with a frown.

"Hawaiian isn't a language. We just say that when we say something like that person looks Hawaiian, or do you want a Hawaiian pizza?"

"Cool. Are they all Hawaiian?"

"Yes," Kahuna said with a smile.

"But wait, that girl Demi, she spoke English."

"Oh, yes. Some of them can speak both English and Polynesian."

"So, who can speak English and Polynesian?" I asked.

"I do not know, actually," Kahuna responded.

"Oh, but aren't you their teacher?" Molly asked.

"Yes, but we all speak the same language to each other."

"But how do we know what they're saying, then?" Molly asked. We were both full of questions.

"I will translate for you."

Molly crossed her arms and frowned. "What does translate mean?"

When she asked that, I felt really smart. "Translate means to say it in English," I said proudly.

"Oh, cool," Molly smiled.

"So, what did Keanu say?" I asked.

"He asked what you were saying."

We all laughed.

"Well, I guess you'll have to translate what I'm saying to him." Kahuna switched modes and started telling the boy different things in Polynesian. The boy—Keanu— nodded his head and said some things to me that I didn't understand.

"He says he's happy you're here and thinks that English is a very interesting language."

"Well, tell him that I think Polynesian is an interesting language too."

Kahuna smiled at me, then looked at Keanu and said another thing to him in Polynesian. After that, we went to the next dancer. She was white and didn't look Hawaiian at all.

"This is Sierra. Her story is fascinating—her mother is Hawaiian, but her father is American."

"Hey, my middle name is Sierra," I said happily.

"How fun," she replied. Everyone else was just as nice.

After we had met them all and were getting ready to go, Molly's disappointment kicked in again. "Well, can we at least go get some ice cream?" she asked.

"Sorry, sweet pea, but it's already two o'clock now, and I told Margaret that we could go to one of the beaches before we have to get going back to the hotel for dinner.

"I'm okay with getting ice cream first," I said with a sparkle in my eye. Dad looked at Mom and grinned.

Chapter 21-We All Scream for Ice Cream

"Oooh, I think I'll get Marzipan, or, oh yeah, I should probably get Cotton Candy," Molly said, inspecting all the different flavours.

"Molly, move over. I can't see," I said as I pushed her aside.

"Girls, make room for each other so you can both see," Mom said.

"There, now I can see a bit better. Wow, look at all the tropical flavours here, Mom. Oh, my goodness, look, there's a dragon fruit flavour? Oooh, and a Mango Pineapple one, too," I said with a glowing face.

"That sounds delicious," Mom replied, peeking over our heads. She used to be able to do that a bit better when we were younger and shorter, but now I was almost as tall as her.

Dad's eyes got huge. "Chocolate Peanut Butter!" he said with crossed eyes.

"We have that at home, Dad," Molly said.

"Yeah, but I still like it. Besides, we have Cotton Candy and Marzipan at home too."

"It could taste different," Molly said in defence.

"Exactly my point," Dad shot back.

Molly shrugged and wisped her hair around her two fingers. She never wins an argument against Dad.

"So, Margaret, what do you think you want?" Dad said.

"I don't know. It all looks so good."

"I know. That's why I was asking you."

I saw Molly lean up towards the counter. "Is she ordering?" I asked.

"I don't know. Molly, are you ordering?"

"Yes," Molly replied as though she was an adult.

"Well, what did you order?" Mom and

I eagerly leaned in.

"Hot Chocolate ice cream."

"But it's hot out, and hot chocolate is hot," I said without thinking.

"What do you think the word ice cream means?"

I guess she had a point. There was no way they could make an ice cream cone hot or even warm.

"Well, I guess you'll have to call it Cold Chocolate then." Mom grinned.

"Why?" Molly asked.

"Um, because it's ice cream, and you can't make a literal hot chocolate ice cream," I said.

"Oh yes, you can," Molly said, resting her elbow on the glass in front of the ice cream.

"How?" I asked.

"You put hot fudge on top," Molly said. She told the waitress to put some hot fudge on it.

"Wow, you really know how to win an argument. Well, unless it's with Dad," I said. I knew that would tick her off.

Molly puffed up one of her bouncy curls and smirked. "I thought as much," I said under my breath.

We all looked over at Dad, who was licking a double-decker ice cream cone. Chocolate dripped down the sides, and peanut butter smudges were already all over his face.

Mom walked over to him and handed him a napkin. "You've got little something on your beard, honey."

Dad frowned. "Isn't that the point of ice cream?"

Mom rolled her eyes and laughed. "You're worse than the girls."

Dad laughed a big belly laugh and then stroked his short beard. "Has my beard already grown back? Why, I just shaved."

"You shaved like a week ago," Mom said as a side note.

"Yeah, that's seven days ago, Dad," Molly added as she licked the side of her drippy ice cream cone.

"Well, I guess I'll have to shave at the hotel."

"I guess so," Mom said as she grabbed a few more napkins for Dad and Molly.

Dad took the napkins from Mom. "Hey, Mol, you wanna have our ice cream outside?" he said.

"Sure," Molly said, linking arms with him.

155

"We'll be out there in a couple of minutes," Mom said as they walked out the door. When they had gone, Mom and I looked at each other. We walked up to the counter. I looked at the flavours one last time to see if I had any last-minute changes.

"You're up first, M.," Mom told me as she pushed me up to the front.

"Thanks a lot, Mom," I said with a laugh.

She smirked, and then I had no choice but to order.

—

I finally decided on Papaya Tangerine with a caramel drizzle. Mom told me to go outside and wait with the rest of the family while she ordered.

When I got outside, Molly and Dad had finished their ice cream and were on their bikes. "Hey, guys, wait up!" I ran over to them. "What are you two doing?"

"We didn't know how long you guys were gonna take, so we decided to have a little bike ride around the block while we were waiting," Molly explained.

"Well, Mom's on her way out right

now. I doubt you'll have time for a bike ride, even a short one."

"Thanks for the head's up, Margaret. We'll ride real fast." Before I could object, Molly zoomed off.

"Oh, no," I said with my hands on my cheeks.

"Don't worry, I'll get her," Dad said.

Mom then came out with an ice cream cone in one hand and a drink carrier with four lemonades in the other hand. I ran over to help her.

"Oh, thanks, sweetie. Where's Molly and Dad?" she asked.

"They went for a quick bike ride because they thought you would be a while."

"Oh no!" Mom said as she passed me a lemonade.

"I told them not to, but Molly wouldn't listen, and she went off without permission. Dad went to get her."

"Okay. Whew. If that's the story, then they'll be back soon. For now, we can have some Mom and daughter time."

"Good, because there's a few things I want to talk to you about."

"Oh, perfect," Mom said, sitting down.

"So, at the airport—"

Dad and Molly interrupted us with their loud calls. "Hey, M.," Dad called as he got off his bike and jogged over to us. "Whatcha got there, Gwen?" he asked, staring with hopeful eyes at the lemonades.

"Just some lemonade," Mom said.

"Yum," Dad said, hinting around.

"Hey, Dad, wait for me." Molly came running up the concrete steps and barged up to Mom. "Oooh, what's that? Can I have some?"

"It's lemonade, and yes, you can both have some." Molly snatched one of the lemonades out of Mom's hand.

"Molly, don't be greedy," Dad said. "There's a verse in the Bible, Psalm 119:36. It says, 'Incline my heart to your testimonies, and not to selfish gain.'"

"Not that you were trying to be selfish or greedy, but it's just something to remember," Mom added.

"How do you guys know all those verses?" Molly asked.

"Because we study the Bible every night before we go to bed, and when we wake up in the morning, your dad and I always read a few verses to start the day," Mom said with a smile.

"Wow," Molly and I said in unison.

"You should always have a time to yourself just spent with you and God," Dad added.

"Maybe I'll try that," Molly said as she tried to take the lid off her lemonade.

Mom smiled. "I think you should, both of you," she said, turning her head in my direction.

I already knew that I wanted to do that. I mean, we went to church, and I went to youth group, and Dad always did devotionals on Saturdays, but I also wanted time to spend soaking in God's Word by myself, too.

"Well, what are we gonna do now?" Molly asked as the whole family watched her yanking at the lid.

"Well, we could go to a beach and have these lemonades," Dad suggested.

"Sounds great," I said, looking at everyone else to see if we all agreed. We all smiled and hopped on our bikes.

Chapter 22 - More Suspicion

When we got to the beach, Molly immediately frantically started searching for her lemonade. I guess she had forgotten about the talk that she had earlier with Mom.

"Here it is," Molly said proudly as she unscrewed the lid. She twisted it and tried to pop it off, but she couldn't seem to get it undone.

"Hey, Mol, ya need some help there?" Dad held his hand out toward her, but Molly didn't seem to want any help.

"Molly Kate Mason never gives up," she said, bearing down on the lid.

"Wow, Mol, your face is getting purple and red," Dad said. He meant it as a joke, but it was kind of true.

"I . . . don't . . . care." Finally, she popped the lid off. "Ah, you see," she said. She took a sip but then spat it out immediately. "Aaakk, what did they put in here? Sugar cubes?"

I turned and laughed. "It can't be that bad. You're just trying to put on a show, aren't you?"

"No! I know I exaggerate sometimes—"

"A lot of times, actually," I cut in.

"Okay, a lot of times, but this time I'm telling the truth. It tastes like their main ingredient was icing sugar."

"Ha. Ha," I said blankly.

"All right then, try it yourself." Molly handed me her drink, but I held my hand out to stop her.

"No, thanks, I'll try my own." I took the lid off my lemonade and held it up to my lips but then stopped to think for a minute. Was Molly telling the truth? Should I believe her? Even though my mind kept telling me to go ahead and drink it, I had to make my own choice.

"Whatcha waitin' for?" Molly asked with crossed arms and a pitchy sound to her Texan accent.

"Will ya just give me a minute?" I said with sideways glances at Molly and the lemonade.

"Fine, but be quick. I wanna watch you spit it out."

Now that got me thinking.

"Umm . . . maybe we should go play volleyball," I said with three blinks.

"Whatever, just make your decision, please." Molly changed her position and took put her hands right on her hips.

In the end, I decided that I needed to taste it for myself. I looked at the lemonade and then at Molly. I held it up to my mouth and took a large gulp. At first, I tasted a slight lemon flavour, but it was immediately followed by a big zap of sugar. I didn't want to look stupid, so I tried to gulp it down in an "It's fine, but not my favourite" way. I finally got it down my throat, there were a few gags along the way, but eventually, it was gone.

"So, how'd it go?" Molly asked as she leaned in to give me an elbow bump.

"Well, it was a lot of sugar. Probably a

lot more than they meant to put in."

"I TOLD you," Molly said pretty loud. A few people even looked over at us.

"Well, it wasn't as dramatic as you made it sound," I shot back, but not as loud.

"You don't have to pretend to be smart in front of me," she said as she flicked a mosquito away from her face. I rolled my eyes and grabbed my water bottle from Dad's backpack.

"All right," I said after I swallowed. "Let's go sit down by the ocean over there." I pointed to a pretty little space near the water. Mom threw her bag over her shoulder, smiled, and grabbed Molly's hand. We made our way over there in a jiffy. Once we were all settled in, Mom took us girls to the bathrooms so that we could change into our swimsuits.

Molly wanted to swim right away. "Mom, can't I please swim right now?"

"Well, not this instant. We're in a bathroom," Mom said with a sarcastic tone.

"You know what I mean," Molly said bluntly.

Mom laughed and put her bag down on a stool. "Only if Margaret wants to go in, too," she said.

"Why?" Molly groaned.

"Because I don't want you going in the ocean all alone. Discussion over."

Molly sighed and stepped outside.

"I'll meet y'all out at the sinks," she said and ran off toward the bathroom exit.

"Why? Where are you going?" Mom asked her as she closed one of the stall doors.

"To use the bathroom," she finally said.

"Okay, but when you're done, please wait at the sinks for us, and don't go sneaking off anywhere."

Molly sighed again. "Yes, ma'am."

When I was done changing into my swimsuit (a yellow one-piece—I had forgotten my bikini at the hotel), I went out to meet Molly by the sinks. At first, I couldn't see where she was because she was curled up on the floor beside a trashcan.

"Molly, what are you doing?" I asked as I tried to pull her up. She wouldn't move, though. She kept stiff.

"Shhh," she said with her finger pressed against her lips. She motioned for me to come down with her, but I wasn't about to sit on the floor by an overflowing trash bin in the middle of Maui.

I shook my head earnestly. "No," I whispered.

"Fine," she whispered back. "Come with me." I don't know why, but I followed her. She led me into one of the stalls and closed the door but didn't lock it.

"What's this all about?" I asked.

"I saw Miss Mary washing her hands," Molly whispered.

"Wow, you have a good eye," I said with a little laugh.

"I just saw Miss Mary, and you're talking about eyes? I think we should be talking about how strange things have been."

"Okay, but I don't think she's a safe person to be around or to be spying on," I said more seriously this time.

"Spying? Do you think I'm a little kid?"

"Technically, you are," I said, dealing things out.

"Doesn't matter. The point I'm trying to make is that I don't spy on people."

"What about that time when you went to go spy on our new neighbours and their hairless cat?"

"I was six, and besides, I didn't actually get to spy on them."

"Why?" I asked.

"Gollum," she said with a shiver.

"Gollum?" I asked, but I stopped in my sentence. I remembered she was talking about their cat and how scary he was.

Just then, Miss Mary opened the door and walked out. Molly let out a silent "Nooo."

I patted her back. "Sorry," I said.

"It's o—" Molly's face turned as white as a sheet.

"What? What is it, sis?" Then I looked over to where she was staring. "Is that really what I think?" Now I'm pretty sure my face was turning white, too.

⁓

Molly and I walked over to what looked like Miss Mary's mini cellphone lying on the sink. Molly picked it up. Then we saw Mom come out of the bathroom wearing her dark purple one-piece swimsuit.

"You girls all set?"

I quickly went to stuff the phone in my pocket, but I realized that I was wearing my swimsuit. I had to think up something real quick.

"Mom," I said. "Can I carry the swim bag for you?"

Mom frowned. "Okay," she said with a confused expression.

Molly and I walked a safe distance behind Mom.

"I put the phone in the bag," I whispered to Molly.

Chapter 23 - Everything Makes Sense Now

When we got back to our spot on the beach, Mom immediately turned onto her back for a suntan. Molly and I went over by the water to "dip our toes in," but really, we were going to take a peek at Miss Mary's mini phone.

I took the phone out of the swim bag and turned it on. "I guess Miss Mary was just washing her hands and dropped her phone by accident," I said.

"Oh, I hope she doesn't have a password," Molly said as she bit her bottom lip until she couldn't stand it.

"She probably will if she's working for a business," I said as I turned on the phone and swiped the screen several times.

"Oh, my word! She does have a password," Molly squealed nervously.

"Don't be a baby. We can figure this out," I said as I nudged her shoulder with mine.

"Right," she said, sitting up a bit straighter. I looked at the screen for a couple of minutes and then turned to face Molly.

"If she works for a business, then maybe the password will have something to do with that," I said, even though I didn't know why I would do that.

"Oooh, good idea! What business does she work for again?" Molly asked.

"I think it was a clothing store," I said, thinking hard.

"Umm, try Old Navy."

"Nice idea, but there's only numbers on here," I said, pointing at the screen.

"Okay, what about a phone number?"

"Good one, but I don't know any phone numbers from clothing stores."

Molly scratched her head. "Well, how are we going to—" She was interrupted by a buzzing sound. "I think her phone's ringing!"

"Oh, dear," I said with my hands planted on both cheeks. "Umm, hang up."

"Let's just see who this person is. Maybe it's the same person that's been calling her all the time," Molly said with a mischievous grin. "The caller ID says 'giddy,'" she read with confusion.

"Well, then, we don't know who it is! Now hang up or give me the phone," I said with a bit of panic.

"No," Molly said and frowned as she tugged it back.

"I need to see who it is."

Through the arguing, one of us accidentally pressed answer.

"Hello?" The voice said.

"Hello," Molly said back.

"Girls?"

Our eyes got huge. Mom was on the other line.

I looked over to where Mom was tanning. She was sitting up and holding her phone against her ear. When she saw us, she hung up and marched over.

"Whaaat is going on?" she asked.

Molly slumped down. Then, things went

from bad to worse. Miss Mary walked over!

Mom turned around. "Mary? Mary! Oh, how are you?"

"Great, I just saw your girls with my phone, so I came over to see what was going on."

"Oh, my goodness, I'm so sorry," Mom said, snatching the phone away from us and handing it over to Miss Mary.

Molly stood up on her tiptoes to look Mom straight in the eyes. "Don't trust her," she said with complete sincerity.

Miss Mary frowned but with a slight smile. "I'm confused. Is she talking about me?"

"Oh no, there must be a misunderstanding," Mom said, looking at us with a horrified expression.

"No, there isn't," Molly insisted. "We heard you in the airport bathroom telling somebody that you were gonna make someone pay. And I've learned in my house that them's fight-startin' words," Molly said without even a slight bit of fear.

Miss Mary started to laugh, and then Mom joined in.

"What? What's so funny?" Molly put her hands on her hips.

"Well, you see Molly," Miss Mary started. "I wasn't trying to hurt anyone; I was talking about the woman that was interviewing me for a new job. She had to literally pay me back for something."

"But we heard you saying that they couldn't find her and that if you—I think—saw her that she should contact you right away. That I heard, and I don't forget things that easy, ya know."

"Again, I wasn't trying to do anything weird. I was having trouble finding my interviewer, so I contacted your mom in case maybe she had seen her. Your mom knows who my interviewer is and what she looks like."

"But . . . but," I said, trying to find my words. "Mom, we already told you that Miss Mary was on the plane and at the airport, but you kept saying that you didn't think she was."

"Oh, Margaret, that's not true. I knew she was there, I just kept saying that she was busy. But I knew. It might've sounded like I didn't believe you girls, but I did."

I sighed and looked down at my toes, resting on the hot sand. I glanced over at Molly, whose head was hanging.

"I was trying to solve a mystery for once," Molly said, sobbing a bit.

"And if you did, what's so great about that?" Mom asked.

"Well, I guess I'd tell my friends that I solved a mystery," Molly replied weakly.

"That's reasonable, but is that the only reason?" I could see that Mom was testing Molly, and I felt tested too.

"Well, umm, I can't really think of any other reasons," Molly replied.

"Girls," Mom said now acknowledging both of us. "We have a problem here. First, the Bible tells us that it's wrong to boast. I mean, it's okay that you would want to tell your friends about solving a mystery, but if that was the only reason, just to brag and boast, then you would be disobeying God.

"Second, you both accused Miss Mary of something that wasn't even true. I'm quite disappointed in you girls, and I expect an apology to Miss Mary."

I felt really bad inside. How could I have accused Miss Mary? She wasn't up to anything.

We looked up at Miss Mary. Her dark hair was wisped in a ponytail. How was I supposed to apologize? I had done something really wrong, and I felt ashamed.

Molly went first. "Miss Mary," she

started out. Then she fell on her knees in the sand with her hands clasped together. "Oh, Miss Mary, please, oh, please forgive us. I was so wrong. You didn't do anything except act a little suspicious, but I don't blame you. We shouldn't have spied on you."

Mom's eyes got large. "Wait, you girls were spying on her?"

Miss Mary cut in. "It's fine, Gwen. Molly, I forgive you."

I walked up to Miss Mary. "Um, ma'am, I just wanted to say first that I should not have accused you of being suspicious or up to something. I feel absolutely awful. I wish I could take back everything that I've done. And I also wanted to ask for your forgiveness."

Miss Mary smiled at us. "Of course, I forgive both of you. I know that you two are very wonderful and that you have learned a lesson."

"Excuse me, Miss Mary. But what job interview were you going to be having?" I asked, trying to brighten things up a bit.

"Oh yes. Actually, you'll find it interesting. I think you're going to like it."

"Really? What is it?" we both asked at the same time.

"She's going to be your new art teacher," Mom said with a smile.

"What!?" we both said at the same time again. Mom explained that the interviewer was from Hawaii and that Miss Mary had to travel there for the interview.

I was just as surprised as Molly was. Ms. Gregory was stepping down, and Miss Mary was going to take her place? I didn't know what to say, but Miss Mary seemed like a nice lady, so I wasn't that worried.

And the rest of the trip was amazing. We saw the hula dancing show, and Miss Mary joined us. We also got to meet Kahuna's sister backstage afterward, and she was really nice.

And in all, it was one of my favourite trips ever—not counting the plane trip home when one of the flight attendants spilled apple juice all over Dad's pants. Ha-ha, don't tell him I said that.

Chapter 24 - Show Your Love

When we got home after the last week of vacation in Hawaii, I was happy to be back but kind of sad that the trip had to end. But a few new things have happened since we got back home.

First of all, Mom and Dad have to take Molly to an eye test soon to see if she needs glasses—I'm not one hundred percent sure when, though. Second, Mom bought Molly and me each a new outfit for the new year of school.

But third is that I was kind of worried about a new year of art class with Miss Mary. Don't get me wrong, I love her. But I'm afraid the story about how we thought Miss Mary was a villain will get out to art class and eventually the whole school. Everyone would be talking about us, and not in the best way.

I knew who would give us the hardest time. Venessa Flytrap.

I know it's not nice to call people names, but this one suits her. She pretends to be nice to kids in front of teachers or even new kids when they first arrive. She doesn't stay nice, though. She traps them, just like a Venus flytrap.

I didn't want to think about Venessa anymore; I didn't even want to think about art class or Miss Mary.

I thought for sure I knew what I was in for this year.

As I got dragged away in my thoughts, I didn't notice that my whole family was trying to wake me up out of my daydreams.

"Margaret," Molly said, nudging my shoulder really hard.

"Margaret Sierra Mason," Mom said, waving her hand in front of my face.

I sat up straight. "Sorry, everyone," I said as I took a big bite of the sandwich in front of me.

Dad grinned. "I guess you fell asleep there for a few minutes."

I shook my head. "I wasn't asleep. I was just thinking."

Molly tilted her head sideways. "What were you thinking about?" she asked.

I bopped my fork on the tip of Molly's nose. "Things," I said, covering up what I felt inside.

Mom and Dad laughed, but Molly pushed my fork away and rubbed her nose.

"Come on, Mol," I said. "It didn't actually hurt."

Molly scowled and chomped on her sandwich harshly. "Why do we even have forks at the table? We're eating sandwiches," she said with her arms in the air.

I set my fork down and grabbed an orange from the fruit bowl in the middle of the table. Mom started a new conversation with Dad about purging our garage this September while Molly and I were in school.

I couldn't help but think about what it would be like having Miss Mary as our new art teacher. I started drifting away again until Molly grabbed her fork and bopped my nose with it like I had done to her. I rubbed it. I guess it had kind of hurt.

Molly grinned and crossed her arms. "Come on, M.," she said, pretending like she was me. "It didn't actually hurt."

I rolled my eyes and pushed her fork away, now pretending like I was her.

"Why do we even have forks at the table? We're eating sandwiches!" I said with a Molly kind of voice.

Molly frowned and turned her chair around. I rubbed my face, then sat up. I knew that Molly was just trying to be funny. Maybe I shouldn't have started a quarrel between us. I had to admit that I hadn't been the nicest sister while we were away. I knew what I had to do.

I gently touched Molly's shoulder. She turned around with watery eyes. I hung my head.

"Molly," I said, taking a deep breath. She nodded and turned her seat back around to face me. I continued, "I feel like I haven't been good to you since we went to Hawaii. I'm really sorry, Mol." I paused and let out a sigh.

Molly shook her head. "It wasn't just you, M. Mom and Dad always say that it takes two to fight."

We smiled and gave each other a big, long hug while Mom and Dad watched. Mom smiled at Dad, "We have two young ladies here, Chris."

We all grinned at one another and finished our sandwiches.

As we ate with happy spirits, all the bad thoughts that I had my mind set on a few minutes ago didn't matter anymore. All that mattered was that we had had an amazing trip, and Molly and I had learned a very big lesson. Most importantly, we have a wonderful Christian family—Mom, Dad, me, and my sister, the Mason family.

Acknowledgments

To my family – thank you for always being there for me, and helping me out with this book. I couldn't have done this without you!

Kori Frazier Morgan – thank you so much for helping me with lots of edits and the countless calls we had putting this book together. You are such an amazing editor!

Max Martin (my big brother) – thank you for accidently deleting my first book a few years ago about snowball the cat. If you hadn't have done that, I might not have written this book.

And to my wonderful Saviour, Jesus – thank you for everything, Lord! You're really the one that let me do this and gave me the gift of telling stories. Thank you for saving my soul and dying for me!

About the Author

Sarah Evangeline Martin is twelve-years-old and lives in Vancouver B.C. with her family. She is the second oldest out of six children—Max, Kate, Silas, Charlie, and Josie Joy. She was ten when she started on this book and it took a few years, but here it is, and she is very thrilled to have it in her hands!

She wants to pursue book writing and is very interested in the film industry, as her family is as well. She has been to many auditions and has been in one flooring commercial in 2018. She hopes that someday, her and her siblings will start a film company and make movies together!

Made in United States
Troutdale, OR
11/14/2023

14554623R10116